INSOMNIA

INSOMNIA

A Novel by
Robert Westbrook

Based on the Screenplay by
Hillary Seitz

**Based on the film *Insomnia*,
directed by Erik Skjoldbjaerg,
written by Nikolai Frobenius
and Erik Skjoldbjaerg**

AN ONYX BOOK

ONYX
Published by New American Library, a division of
Penguin Putnam Inc., 375 Hudson Street,
New York, New York 10014, U.S.A.
Penguin Books Ltd, 80 Strand,
London WC2R 0RL, England
Penguin Books Australia Ltd, Ringwood,
Victoria, Australia
Penguin Books Canada Ltd, 10 Alcorn Avenue,
Toronto, Ontario, Canada M4V 3B2
Penguin Books (N.Z.) Ltd, 182–190 Wairau Road,
Auckland 10, New Zealand

Penguin Books Ltd, Registered Offices:
Harmondsworth, Middlesex, England

First published by Onyx, an imprint of New American Library,
a division of Penguin Putnam Inc.

First Printing, May 2002
10 9 8 7 6 5 4 3 2 1

PUBLISHER'S NOTE
This is a work of fiction. Names, characters, places, and incidents either are
the product of the author's imagination or are used fictitiously, and any
resemblance to actual persons, living or dead, business establishments,
events, or locales is entirely coincidental.

ONE

Will Dormer opened his eyes abruptly. He had been dozing, lulled by the hypnotic high-pitched drone of the Cessna floatplane. Below him, the land was immense, a frozen moonscape. They were flying over a glacier, a dazzling mountain of barren ice. Alaska! It was beautiful, he supposed. But no place for a cop from balmy L.A.

He wasn't sure what had woken him. A memory? A dream? *Blood on a shirt cuff, a stain that will never come clean, though you scrub at it forever.* Blinking himself awake, Will felt jumbled. With an effort, he brought his eyes back inside the cabin and focused his attention on the file that was open in his lap. There was a photograph of a dead girl, naked and bruised. She was very young, only a teenager, hardly more than a child. It was terrible to die so young, with all of life's promises unfulfilled. Murder was familiar to Will Dormer, but it still had the power to upset him.

Dormer glanced over to Hap Eckhart in the seat next to him, wondering how his partner was going to survive their Alaskan exile. Hap was forty-five, no kid, but there was something eternally boyish about him—an L.A. boy, California to the max, good-looking and slick, savvy of city streets and ways. At the moment, Hap was nodding to himself, staring out the window on his side of the plane with a look of bemused astonishment on his face, fascinated to find himself in a place where there wasn't a single freeway or burrito stand or Korean takeout anywhere in sight.

"Jesus, I thought we had a population problem," Hap shouted over the engine. "Everyone should just move up here!"

Will shook his head and looked meaningfully at the file in his lap. The dead girl. But Hap was intent on playing tourist. He reached over and tapped the glass on Will's side of the crowded cabin. "Just look at it!" he cried, pointing at the panorama of sky and ice.

"We're not on vacation, Hap."

"Nothing wrong with smelling the roses."

It was a typical Hap remark. "Tell that to *her*, partner," Will said moodily, nodding at the grim photograph. He felt irritated by everything around him—violent death, his partner's good nature, and this huge alien land. He was probably only being uptight. That was another word Hap liked to bandy about: uptight. In California, the good life was still the dream of the increasingly teeming masses. And to enjoy the good life, a person was supposed to relax, get with the groove, smell the roses.

The Cessna lurched, bouncing over violent currents of air. The pilot turned back in his seat to see how his city passengers were making out.

"Better hang on," he said. "We're heading into some more of the rough stuff." The pilot was a military type with a rugged, outdoorsy face. Will found himself disliking anyone who looked quite so healthy and chipper. The pilot's name was Spencer and he appeared the sort of guy who could make a fire without matches, catch a string of trout for breakfast, and shoot a bear for dinner. But apparently murder made him squeamish. Will saw that the pilot's eyes had wandered to the faxed photo in his lap of the dead naked girl. The plane bounced again, violently enough to make the sandwich Will had eaten in the Anchorage airport do a sickening flip-flop in his stomach. The Cessna was going crazy in the sky, and still the pilot couldn't take his damn eyes off the girl!

"Shouldn't you be watching the road?" Hap asked.

Reluctantly, Spencer returned his attention to his instrument panel and joystick and the business of flying the plane. He would have a story to tell his bar buddies, how he flew these two L.A. cops on some mission from hell. Maybe he would dream of the dead girl, as Will had, imagining her in life, smiling and full of eager youth. The Cessna banked hard to the left, clearing the glacier and climbing over a range of densely wooded mountains. In the distance, the mountains plunged down toward the dazzling blue beyond the Alaskan coastline, an ocean that bore little resemblance to the citified surf at Santa Monica.

The Last Frontier—that was what people called this wild land. Will closed his eyes and felt suddenly tired and old. He wasn't certain he was up for Alaska. There was only one frontier left for tired cops such as himself who had been living on the edge for too many years, but it wasn't a final frontier he cared much to contemplate.

The floatplane descended sharply, circled a wide protected bay, and landed, skimming across the bright cold water.

TWO

Detective Ellie Burr was entirely too young. Greener than green, brand-new. Her great fear was that she would come off as a real hick to the big-city cops and that they wouldn't take her seriously.

She watched from the end of the landing dock as the floatplane circled, came in on a final approach, then glided down upon the water like some huge dragonfly setting down. The "airport," such as it was, consisted of the bay, the dock, and a small shack on the end of the dock, which served as an office. A sign swung in the wind: NIGHTMUTE, ALASKA. HALIBUT FISHING CAPITAL OF THE WORLD. Ellie wondered how all this would appear to two cops from Los Angeles. Nervous and excited, she smoothed her vest and made certain the gold shield on her belt was clearly visible. Ellie Burr needed all the props at her disposal to let the world know she was a real honest-to-God detective. She was twenty-three years old, petite with short brown hair. On good days, she considered herself pretty, though not stunningly so—not like the girls they had on the beaches in California. On bad days, she was afraid she looked . . . well, like a chipmunk.

"Eleanor? What are you doing here?"

Unfortunately, Ellie recognized the voice calling to her. She turned and saw an old man hosing down the side of the shack at the head of the dock. It was Mr. Angstrom, about the last person she wanted to see at a time when she needed every shred of dignity.

"Hey, Mr. Angstrom!" she called back. "Police business."

He grinned. "Didn't you used to baby-sit for us?"

"Don't baby-sit anymore, sir," she informed him, refusing to be riled. "Made detective three weeks ago."

His grin got bigger. He seemed to think this was quite the joke. "Boy. Charlie shorthanded down at the station?"

Ellie shook her head pleasantly and turned back to the floatplane, watching as it pulled up to the dock. She was accustomed to people not taking her seriously. It bothered her, but it was a challenge as well, bringing out a streak of sheer stubbornness in her nature. The inhabitants in Nightmute were more than a little behind the times when it came to gender roles, especially the guys.

The Cessna's twin engines coughed and died. With the plane quiet, you could hear once again the natural sounds of wind and water, the sounds of the Alaska she so loved. Spencer, the pilot, climbed out of his door, jumped on the dock, and tied up. When the plane was secure, he opened the rear door, letting his passengers out. The two cops were unsteady on their feet as they climbed out of the small plane. No one would mistake them for locals, not dressed in suits, city clothes, and shiny shoes.

Ellie recognized Detective Will Dormer immediately from photographs she had seen of him. He had a face that must have been handsome once, but now was like a map of life experience—and clearly not all of those experiences had been good. He looked haggard, skeptical, and keen. Fiftyish, maybe older. Thin, almost gaunt. Nevertheless, Ellie found him attractive. The man alongside him was younger and better-looking, but to Ellie he did not have the same appeal.

Detective Dormer had just spotted the swinging sign. "Halibut fishing capital of the world!" he read aloud, not with sarcasm, but as though the idea of fishing for halibut was beyond human comprehension. Ellie took a deep breath to settle her nerves and walked across the dock to greet him.

"Detective Dormer!" she said enthusiastically. She reached to take his bag, then shook hands with him vigorously. "It's an honor to meet you! Detective Ellie Burr."

The L.A. detective gave her a look that was inscrutable but polite. He did not appear overcome with enthusiasm to be there. He turned to introduce the younger man, who had stepped off the plane with a newspaper folded under his arm, which impressed Ellie as extremely cosmopolitan.

"My partner—"

"Detective Eckhart!" she interrupted, wanting them both to know that she was well prepared. "Welcome to Nightmute." Ellie led them up the dock to where her Jeep Cherokee was parked with its Nightmute Police Department logo on the door. Down the street, the pulp mill was belching smoke into the sky, a cloud of pollution that hung against the mountains. Nightmute was not a tourist mecca. It was only a small, bleak Alaskan town with a main street and strip malls and low buildings—nothing to put on a postcard. She wondered if the two men from California would be disappointed. But of course, they had not come there for the sights.

She put their bags into the back of the Jeep. "I just want to say how incredible it is to have you working with us, Detective Dormer. I've followed all your cases. Theodore Dineli, Frank Prud'homme, the Ocean Park shootings, and especially the Leland Street murders. That was my case study at the academy."

She saw a look pass between the two men. Silently, Will slipped into the front passenger seat, while Hap Eckhart got into the rear. Ellie started up the Jeep and lurched away. She knew she was talking too much, practically gushing. But she couldn't help herself. After all, she didn't meet famous big-city detectives every day.

Ellie glanced over at Will and saw there was a long scar on his neck. "That's where Ronald Langley cut you in the basement of 325 Leland, isn't it?"

Will Dormer didn't seem to know what to make of her. "Did your homework, Detective," he said finally in a quiet voice.

Ellie's smile was close to ecstatic. "The Leland Street murders was my case study at the academy."

Had she said that already? She forced herself to shut up. *Not one more gushing word!* They drove along the outskirts of town, past rambling warehouses and lines of quaint stores. The two men stared out their windows and didn't say anything. Not a single question about the fishing or how the winters were, or what it was like to live here—the usual questions outsiders asked. Nor did they speak about the case.

"We'll drop your bags at the Lodge," she told them.

"Let's get to the station," Will suggested. Actually, it was more than a suggestion—it was a command.

Ellie glanced over to him. He was staring gloomily at a fishing-and-tackle store across the street; it had a huge stuffed halibut in the window. They probably didn't have stores like that in Los Angeles.

"Right. You want to get started," she agreed. "Most homicides are solved by work done in the first seventy-two hours."

Will's face softened and he granted Ellie a very slight, wan smile. "Forty-eight," he corrected. "We're a day behind."

THREE

The Nightmute Police Department was located in a one-story gray building that was generically modern. From the outside, it could have been an insurance company, or a place where you paid your electric bill, maybe even a bank—anything, it seemed to Detective Will Dormer, except what it actually was. He reminded himself to be open-minded. After all, this wasn't L.A. He was having himself a new experience here. Meanwhile, he shouldn't judge a book by its cover.

The girl, Detective Ellie Burr—to Will, she looked hardly old enough to drive, much less be a cop—led them into the interior of the station to Chief Charlie Nyback's office. Hap took up the rear, clutching a copy of the *L.A. Times* under his arm as if it were some talisman of city life that might protect him here in the sticks. Chief Nyback was sitting behind a cluttered desk with a window behind him showing the pulp mill in the distance. Will had met Charlie Nyback a number of years back. He was a good old boy, Alaskan style: a big, comfortable man with gray hair and shrewd eyes. He had a green army sweater over his police uniform.

Charlie stood up from his desk and smiled. He limped across the room and gave Will a shake and a slap on the back. There was some story about Charlie's limp, a hunting accident involving a bear—Will forgot the details, but it added to the folksy aura of the man.

"How you doing, Charlie?" Will asked.

"Hey, Charlie," Hap managed.

"Christ, haven't seen you boys since . . ." The chief paused, searching his memory.

"Just after Leland Street," Will prompted.

"What's that, then?"

"Seven years," Will told him.

"Eight," Hap corrected.

Charlie seemed to think this was big news. "Seven years! Shit." He sighed, pondering the mortality of time. He turned to the girl detective in the doorway. "Get everyone into the bull pen, Ellie." He spoke to her in a fatherly voice—a tone that would have gotten him a million-dollar lawsuit for egregious paternalism had he dared use it on a female cop in Los Angeles.

Will watched Ellie back out of the room, as if she were afraid to turn around and miss anything. Frankly, he was starting to find her youth just a little exhausting. "Nice kid," he said.

"Loves the job," Charlie agreed, limping back to his desk. "When I called Buck for advice on this, I never thought he'd actually send you guys up." He sat down and gave Will a questioning look. The man might be country, but he was no fool. His eyes shifted from Will to the headline on Hap's *L.A. Times*. Will knew what the headline said without looking: DEEPER INVESTIGATION INTO ROBBERY HOMICIDE. Charlie paused, not wanting to be indelicate. But he had to ask. "Something to do with that bullshit you got going on down at Robbery Homicide?"

Hap started to explain. "They're moving in, Charlie—"

"It's nothing," Will interrupted. "Usual crap. Buck just figured you could—"

"They got Finn and Kentor on narcotics theft," Hap went on. "Corelli on unwarranted shooting. Now the fuckers are wading through files, looking for headlines."

Will was irritated at his partner for talking about the sorry mess they had left behind. "It'll blow over," he said, giving Hap a significant look, closing the subject.

Chief Nyback fingered a piece of paper from his

desk and gave Will a long look. "Got a message here from a guy named Warfield."

"I.A.'s pit bull," Will explained. He tried to sound casual, but this was not good news.

"Wants to be posted on your movements," Charlie continued. He paused a beat, studying his two California visitors. Then, ceremoniously, he crumpled the message and dropped it into the trash. He stood abruptly, picked up a file from his desk, and began limping toward the door. "You'll find things more straightforward up here. Good guys, bad guys. A lot less public relations. Simple."

Charlie paused by his door and a cloud seemed to pass over his face. "Except for this," he said, holding up the file he had taken from his desk. He silently mouthed a name. Will was no lip-reader, but it was a name he knew. The dead girl. *Kay Connell.*

Chief Nyback led Will and Hap down a hallway. "We get our share of crazies, stuck in the middle of nowhere," he was saying. Will could imagine how that would be true in the vast, unimaginable emptiness of land. No distractions for a sick mind ticking away. "But it's predictable passions, you know? This is different. Cold, methodical."

Charlie opened a door and led them into the bull pen, the common area of the station, a large open room that was crowded with desks, computers, telephones, filing cabinets, and an impressive gun cabinet against a far wall. There were three men lounging in various attitudes behind their desks. Two of the men were in uniform, but the third, a guy in his early thirties with a retro seventies mustache and sideburns, was dressed in what passed in Alaska for plain clothes—boots, jeans, and a spiffy, well-ironed cowboy shirt. The boots, at this moment, were resting very casually on his desk. He seemed to be making a statement. Detective Ellie Burr stood in the back of the room and did not appear to be part of the male camaraderie.

Chief Nyback did the introductions. "Detectives Dormer and Eckhart, on loan from Buck Lundgard, Los Angeles Robbery and Homicide. They'll be helping with the Connell case. . . ."

The plainclothes cop took his boots from his desk. "*Helping?*" He didn't seem much to like the idea.

"And we're damn lucky to have 'em," Nyback continued, speaking to the room at large. "Anything they need to see, you show them. Anywhere they want to go, you take them." He gestured finally at the plainclothes cop. "This is Detective Fred Duggar. He's been heading up the investigation."

Will got the picture, picking up the whiff of hostility. The last thing he wanted was to invade the sacred turf of Detective Fred Duggar, with his manly facial hair. He nodded at the detective and offered his hand. Duggar hesitated just long enough to let Will know he didn't shake hands with just any old asshole who happened to wander there from the Lower Forty-eight. Then he offered a brief, reluctant clasp.

Will was not there to socialize. "Let's get right on it," he suggested.

"You've seen what we got?" Fred asked.

"Yeah. Let's start with the body."

"You got the report?"

Will felt a new wave of resistance, as if the report had everything covered and further investigation was a waste of time. The world was composed, he supposed, of people holding on for dear life to their petty prerogatives. "I need to see her for myself," he persisted.

A short while later, Detective Fred Duggar and Detective Ellie Burr led Will and Hap out of the station into the department parking lot. Fred spent some time adjusting a baseball cap on his head at just the right angle. Will was starting to get bored with the guy. He walked briskly toward the Cherokee, hoping Fred would get the idea that they had more important things to do than play head games with one another.

Fred saw where Will was headed and stopped him. "We can walk from here." Without waiting for an answer, Fred sauntered off across the lot, in the opposite direction from the Cherokee. He called out behind him, "If that's fast enough for you."

Will glanced over at Hap, raising an eyebrow.

Hap shrugged. "Alaskan hospitality."

Detective Duggar and Detective Burr were already halfway across the parking lot, walking with long country strides. Hap followed after them, and Will took up the rear. There was an acrid smell in the air from the pulp mill factory that mixed with an underlying aroma of dead fish and salt water. Will Dormer was getting an increasingly bad feeling about small-town life on the Last Frontier.

FOUR

The morgue was located in the basement of St. Francis Hospital. The temperature was kept cool, as these places always were to discourage the growth of bacteria, and there was a sharp chemical smell of formalin in the air that did not entirely conceal the scent of body putrefication and decay. Death was a messy business, despite the best efforts of science.

Will studied the young woman on the stainless-steel table. Kay Connell. It was important to know the dead by name, to hold off as long as possible the forgetful anonymity of nonexistence. *Kay* ... an old-fashioned name, a remnant of an Anglo mid-America that was quickly disappearing from cities like Los Angeles. *Kay Connell.* Hard syllables for parents to put upon a baby girl.

The coroner was an elderly woman, perhaps as old as seventy. She had gray hair and a stern expression. She reminded Will of a piano teacher he'd had as a kid, what seemed like a few lifetimes ago, who had been sorely disappointed because he never practiced. The lady coroner gave him a recital of information. "Clear cause of death was herniation of the brain stem due to intracerebral hemorrhage. . . ."

Will was accustomed to such medical terms—those long words were the litany of death. But at the moment he was looking for something more human in the dead girl on the table. He was relieved that Fred and Ellie were hanging back, staying close to Hap, giving Will room to . . . what? *Imagine*. That was what it boiled down to. To see this girl and try to imagine her life.

She had been seventeen years old. A pretty girl, auburn hair, tall and well shaped. There was something ethereal about her. Poetic, if that wasn't imagining too much, even lying naked and inert on a cold stainless-steel table. Boys—men, perhaps—would have found her attractive. Someone, of course, had wished her violent harm. She had red bruises that blossomed across her neck and shoulders and breasts. Will pointed at the marks, getting the coroner's attention.

"These contusions?"

"Superficial," she told him.

Will moved closer to the body, studying in

minute detail the marks on her neck. He could imagine a hand lashing out, striking Kay on her neck. *But whose hand?*

"Most of the trauma was to her face and the top of her neck," the coroner added.

Will shifted his focus to the girl's face. Had she had time to scream? Yes, he was certain she had. This death was not quick. Even now, her face was a map of horror.

"Signs of rape?" Hap asked.

"No," said the coroner.

Will noticed something that surprised him. He leaned in closer, examining a bruise on Kay's upper arm. At the outer rim of the bruise, there was a hint of yellow.

"This one covers an older bruise," he said quietly. Almost reverently.

The coroner nodded and pointed to another place on Kay's neck. "There's an older one here, too."

"They're both in the report," Fred put in from the sidelines.

Will ignored Fred Duggar and his report. He drifted slowly around the table. His movements were calm and deliberate. He had great respect for the dead; he knew they were trying to speak to him, tell him what he needed to know. Very gently, he lifted Kay's hair in his hand. He leaned forward, closed his eyes, and inhaled the scent of the hair. When he opened his eyes, he caught Ellie staring at him in astonishment.

"He washed her hair," Will told her.

Very carefully he picked up Kay's hand. It was a delicate hand, pale as alabaster, heavy in death. He examined the fingers and frowned.

"Scrubbed her nails!" he added.

"It's all in the report, Detective," Fred said wearily.

Very carefully, Will laid Kay's dead hand back on the table.

"The report didn't say that he clipped them, too."

"She could've clipped them herself," suggested the coroner.

Will gestured at the girl's hand. "No polish on the ends of the nails. *She* had them painted. Someone else cut them short."

He moved around to her feet. The others in the room watched while he carefully spread the girl's toes.

"Her toes, too." Will had never encountered anything quite like this.

"Naked when you found her?" Hap asked Fred.

The detective nodded. "Last seen wearing a red paisley dress."

Will backed away from the table and stared at the dead girl intently, willing her to life. He could almost imagine her in her red paisley dress, laughing. It broke his heart somehow. Her body had been found stuffed in a garbage bag on top of a trash heap outside of town, a final indignity.

"No fibers? Flakes? Hairs?" Hap was asking the coroner.

The gray-haired woman shook her head.

Fred had to throw in his two cents of attitude. "We know about forensics up here. I told you—the body gave us nothing."

Nothing? Will continued to stare at the dead girl, deep in his own thoughts. Finally, he blinked and the spell seemed to be broken. "She gave us plenty," he said aloud. He turned to Hap. "All this trouble. All this care. Why?"

Hap shrugged.

"He knew her," Ellie suggested, emboldened to speak.

Will glanced at the young detective, surprised and pleased. He gave her a small nod. "He knows we can connect him to her."

"So this isn't some random psycho? Crime of passion?" Fred asked. It was obvious from his tone that this was his theory of the case.

Will turned back toward Kay Connell's broken body, tilting his head to see her better. "Maybe," he agreed. "But whatever happened, his *reaction* wasn't passionate. He didn't panic. Didn't try to chop her up or burn her beyond recognition. Just thought about what we'd look for, and calmly removed all those traces. No haste, no rush."

"Cold," Hap said.

"Oh, yeah."

"But why would he clip the nails after he scrubbed them?" Ellie asked.

It was a good question. Will thought for a moment. "Manipulating the body. Prolonging the moment."

"No mutilation," Hap pointed out.

"Not this time."

"You think there've been others?"

Will shook his head. "But there will be. He crossed a line and didn't even blink. How do you come back from that?" He pulled off his latex autopsy gloves, faintly stained with the girl's blood. "Let's find out who Kay was," he said decisively. He turned to Fred Duggar. "I want to see where she lived."

Fred nodded, chastened. For once, he didn't have the nerve to mention his report. As for Ellie Burr, she seemed to be taking mental notes, memorizing every moment for some future examination where she would have to get every question right.

FIVE

Kay Connell had lived with her mother in a one-story house on a small lot on a residential street that was within walking distance of what passed in Nightmute for downtown. It was a house that aspired to the American dream, but hadn't quite arrived.

There was a front porch with a swing that reminded Will of the Midwest—a Midwest strangely transplanted to Alaska. Everything was clean, but a little shabby. The furniture looked as if it had come from a thrift shop. As for Mrs. Connell, she was a tight, tall woman with haunted eyes who might have been pretty back in high school, but life hadn't been especially kind to her. There was no sign of any Mr. Connell. From Fred Duggar's report, Will knew that there had been a divorce about ten years earlier.

Mrs. Connell met them at the front door and led them over a worn carpet down a hallway. It was the sort of house where everything rattled when you walked—dishes, windows, vases on tables. Of course, they accounted for a lot of footsteps: Will, Hap, Fred, and Ellie in the rear.

"Fred told me not to touch anything, so I haven't tidied up," Mrs. Connell told them. She stopped at her daughter's closed door, her hand hesitating on the knob. "She hates it when I go in her room, anyway."

Mrs. Connell put her hand to her mouth as she realized the tense she had just used. A present tense that was forever gone. She looked momentarily so brittle Will was afraid she would break. He touched her arm, comforting. Her body was rigid as a statue.

"Thank you, Mrs. Connell." He tried to express sympathy, yet dismiss her at the same time. The last thing he wanted was a mother on the verge of a breakdown watching over them as they went through her dead daughter's possessions.

The woman turned and floated down the hall toward the kitchen. *Like a ghost*, Will thought, *some creature lost between worlds.*

Will stood in the girl's room and tried to absorb her. You knew right away that this was the private realm of a teenage girl. There was something fluffy about the decor. Shag carpeting on the floor and clouds painted on the ceiling. There were magazine covers taped to the walls, pictures of rock stars Will had never heard of. Shelves of CDs by the same rock stars, music of a generation so far removed from Will's that they might have lived on different planets. Yet teenagers in America were a constant, creations of the media for mass consumption. Styles changed, but the emotional heart remained the same.

"She went to a party Friday night?"

"Not exactly a party," Ellie answered. "A local dive where the kids hang out."

Will pulled open a chest of drawers. There were underwear, panties and bras and other girlish things. He rooted around through T-shirts and shorts and socks. Bright colors. The sort of clothes you bought on sale at Wal-Mart or JCPenney.

"No diary?"

"Didn't find one, but her mother says she kept a journal."

Will turned his attention to the junk on top of the bureau: a brush, lipstick, earrings, a pencil, loose change, and an unframed photograph of Kay smiling awkwardly into the camera, her hair blowing across her face. It was good to see Kay Connell very much alive. But the photograph was torn in two and half of it was missing. It looked to Will as if she had been standing next to someone, but whoever that someone was, he or she had been deliberately removed.

Will stepped back and looked around. He saw a wastebasket in the corner, half full. He upended it onto the carpet, knelt, and began sifting through the trash. There were candy wrappers, an empty lipstick container, crumpled-up attempts to write an English essay. And finally the other half of the photograph. Will studied it carefully. He had been expecting to find a boy, maybe some heartbreaker she had decided to cast away in a fit of anger. But the torn picture showed a girl—a pretty girl with white-blond hair who was laughing and looking a great deal less self-conscious than Kay had appeared in her half of the picture.

"Who's this?" He held up the photograph.

Ellie squinted, leaning forward to see. "Tanya Franke. Kay's best friend."

"I want to talk to her."

Will studied the photo of Kay, burning her image into his mind, trying to make her real, bring her back to life. What had she been thinking? There was a suggestion of trouble in her eyes that was in marked contrast to the carefree expression on the face of her best friend Tanya, who had ended up in the wastebasket. Something had been weighing on Kay. Will slipped the picture into his coat pocket and turned to Ellie and Fred.

"Who was Kay Connell?" he asked.

Neither Hap, nor Fred, nor Ellie knew how to respond.

"Was she popular?" Will demanded. "Did she like this town, or was she gonna move on, first chance she got?"

He moved to the dead girl's closet and opened the door. "What were her dreams? Her vices?" He began going through her clothes, running his hands along dresses and blouses, skirts and jackets—nice, but mass-produced, made with cheap materials. "She knew this guy. If we know her, we can know him."

Will's fingers stopped. He had just touched a different kind of fabric, something soft and shimmery and fine. He pulled out a small black dress with spaghetti straps that was different from any of the other clothes in Kay's wardrobe. The dress was elegant and costly, not something you'd pick up off the rack at a huge box store. Will looked for the label but it had been cut off.

"This is designer. Expensive." He looked over to Fred. "The boyfriend, Randy?"

"Randy Stetz," Fred confirmed.

"Could he afford this?"

"He's still in high school," Ellie said.

Will put the dress back in the closet and glanced around the room. Kay had done her best to create a hip teenage pad for herself with limited resources. But there was no hiding the fact that the room was small and shabby.

"Well, her mother didn't buy it," he said.

"What are we thinking?" Hap asked as he looked around. He spotted a man's necktie, and called Will's attention to it.

Will didn't answer. His eyes kept scanning the room. Had he missed anything? He focused on the bedside table. There was a heart-shaped jewelry box, very feminine. He opened the box and pulled out a finely wrought silver necklace. It was very pretty. Like the elegant black dress in the closet, the necklace was obviously costly, different from Kay's other belongings, showing a more sophisticated taste. The black dress and the necklace simply didn't fit with the rest of the teenage clutter and memorabilia in the room.

"No stepfather?" Will asked. "Rich uncle?"

"Nope," Fred said.

Will held the necklace up to the window. It sparkled, catching the daylight.

"An admirer?" he wondered. He turned to Fred. "I need to talk to the boyfriend."

"I can get him to the station."

"No. Let's pull him out of class, right in front of his friends. Catch him off guard, get everyone talking." Will put the necklace back inside the heart-shaped jewelry box and started for the door. "How far's the high school?"

He saw Fred throw an amused look at Ellie. She cleared her throat. "It's ten o'clock, Detective Dormer."

Will stared at her. He didn't understand.

"At *night*," she told him.

Will was confused. He turned toward the bedroom window. Outside it was bright as day. He sighed, remembering where he was.

"When's it get dark around here?"

"It doesn't," Fred told him. "Not this time of year."

Will shook his head. This wasn't normal. In fact, as far as Will Dormer was concerned, this was goddamn weird. He wondered how people slept in a place like Alaska where night was nearly the same as day.

SIX

The lobby of the Pioneer Lodge was built of wood and stone, with a high cantilevered roof. It was clean yet rustic, no different from a million other Triple-A recommended motels in rural America. There were displays of tourist brochures on the counter advertising fishing trips, horseback riding, and a Santa's village that no family should miss. Outside the window, Will could see a giant wooden sculpture of a bear, rearing up on its two hind feet. Downstairs, in a corner of the lower floor, there was a restaurant and bar.

Will and Hap approached the reception desk, where they found a woman behind a computer dunking a tea bag into a mug. She was in her late thirties, an attractive woman with intelligent eyes, not much makeup, dressed in jeans and a light sweater that showed her figure to advantage. *Down home* was the term Will would have used to describe her. Country pretty. She smiled at them.

"Lower Forty-eight," she said.

Hap looked at her more closely. "Lower Forty-eight?"

"You're not from here. I can tell by your walk."

A piece of plastic on the counter said that her name was Rachel Clement. Hap smiled at her warmly. "Oh? How's that?"

"Unsure," she told them.

Rachel Clement looked like she was going to expand on this theme, how an Alaskan native could spot a visitor five miles away, but Will cut in. "Dormer and Eckhart," he said. "We have a reservation."

She studied Will longer than a reception person at a motel usually studies someone. Then she moved to her computer.

"Don't be fooled by my friend's frivolous demeanor," Hap told her, flirting. "Inside he's all business."

Rachel smiled politely as she found their reservation in the computer and gave them a card to fill out. Hap did all the writing, and left an imprint on a credit card that would be billed to the L.A.P.D.

"Restaurant still serving?" Will asked her.

Rachel glanced up at the clock on a wall by the front door. "Kitchen's about to close."

Will took their key. "We'll be quick."

Hap smiled at Rachel, putting on a thousand watts of sunny California charm, doing his best to make an impression. But it was Will that Rachel's eyes followed as the two men walked away.

Nouvelle cuisine had not yet migrated up the coast from California to the Pioneer Lodge Bar and Restaurant in Nightmute, Alaska. Will and Hap read their way through huge Naugahyde padded menus. There was not a single froufrou pasta, or salad with raspberry-balsamic vinaigrette, or chicken breast with a sundried tomato pesto sauce.

But there was plenty of fish. Hap read aloud, in disbelief, "Halibut Calabrese. Halibut Olympia. Halibut Cajun style . . ."

"Can't wait to see what's for dessert," Will sighed. He took a healthy sip of his bourbon and water. The restaurant was lined with dark wood paneling and Alaskan memorabilia on the walls, stuffed fish and antlers and signed photographs of men on their boats. There were large windows with long, heavy drapes closed against the light, which was seeping in around the edges. The restaurant adjoined the bar and Will could see a few rough-looking guys on stools, crouching over their beer. As he looked, a huge specimen in a red lumber jacket and baseball cap locked eyes with him, sending out waves of hostility. Maybe he didn't like visitors from the Lower Forty-eight.

Maybe he didn't like anyone at all. Will stared back, refusing to give ground.

"Looks like the natives are restless," Will said, enjoying himself in some odd way. Two stags clashing horns. Or maybe it was moose that clashed up here. Most likely, any male animal would do.

Hap put his menu down. From the side of his vision, Will could see him fidget with a corner of the menu. He appeared to be unsettled, which was unusual for Hap, a guy who lived in the perpetual comfort zone.

"We gotta talk," Hap told him.

"No, we don't."

Nevertheless, Will broke off eye contact with the redneck gorilla in the bar and turned toward his partner.

"Still just wanna sit tight?" Hap asked.

"Why not? Nothing's changed."

Hap took a deep breath. *"Nothing's changed?"* Sarcasm dripped from his voice. "The fuck you think we're doing in the halibut fishing capital of the world, Will?"

"Buck figured Charlie could use some—"

It was the start of a lie, and Hap wouldn't let him finish. "Buck figured I.A. was gonna come to me next." Hap lowered his eyes. "And he was right. Warfield had me locked in his office for three hours yesterday, Will. *Three hours!*"

Will studied his partner. Warfield was the current hotshot of Internal Affairs, an ambitious shit-head of the first degree. But not a real threat, as long as they closed ranks. As long as partners remained partners.

"Just rattling your cage, pal," Will assured him.

"Well, it's rattling hard. Look, I never made a secret of stuff I did back when it was me and Finn." Will leaned forward and lowered his voice. "Hap, they got *nothing*."

"The fuckers are all over me, Will!" Hap studied his hands on the table. "Me and Trish talked it through. I'm sorry . . . but I gotta cut a deal."

Will stared at his partner with contempt. If Hap cut a deal with Internal Affairs, a lot of things were going to fall apart, starting with Will's career.

Hap looked up, pleading. "Will, I got a family. Warfield made it clear I could get probation—"

"Don't even say this shit, Hap!"

"You're not gonna be involved."

"'Course I'm gonna be fucking involved!"

Hap shook his head. "You're a goddamned hero! With your reputation—"

"My *reputation* is the whole problem!" Will kept his voice down but he felt like screaming. "You think Warfield gives a flying fuck about you and Finn shaking down drug dealers?"

Hap stared back, his mouth flapping, surprised that Will knew so much.

Will nodded, pressing his point. "You think *that's* gonna get him his headlines? He needs his big fish, Hap, and that's me. He's putting the squeeze on *you* to get to *me*, understand?"

"But you're clean, Will. He can't—"

"I do my job well. But it's a *complex* job. Do it long enough, there'll be something there. Something they can use to get at your credibility."

"Bullshit," Hap said. "They got nothing on you 'cause there's nothing to get."

Will fixed his partner with a burned gaze. "What about *Dobbs*?"

Hap blinked and didn't look happy. He glanced around the bar, glanced anywhere so he would not have to meet Will's hard stare.

"That's *different*," he managed. "Even Warfield doesn't want shit like that back on the street."

"Oh, yeah?" Will's voice was bitter. "You figure that out chatting to him in his fucking office, Hap? Good guy, yeah? Good cop? Trust him?"

Hap shrugged and all pretense of shame fell away. It was like a mask had fallen off to reveal the real Hap Eckhart underneath. "Chance I gotta take, pal," he said smoothly.

Will supposed he had always known Hap didn't give a shit for anyone except numero uno. Still, he softened his voice for one more try.

"Come on, Hap, tough it out. I won't lie to you. You'll take some heat. But nothing you can't handle. It's not you they want—it's me. Don't fucking cave. That's just what they're waiting for."

Hap stared back, unmoved, unrepentant. "Sorry."

Will felt total disgust. "You know what you're doing? Think of all the cases that depended on my *word*. My *judgment*. The house of cards comes tumbling down. All these fuckers back on the streets."

"Will, you don't *understand*. You don't have a family."

"We're *cops*, Hap. We took on a greater responsibility," Will told him bitterly. "It's not just about us. A whole lot of people depend on us. People with families. To help them. Vindicate them. Protect them. That's what I've spent my life doing. You're gonna destroy it. And for what? So some I.A. prick gets one step closer to chief of police, or playing golf with the mayor, or whatever the fuck he's after."

"You finished? I'm sorry," Hap said with a shrug, but he really wasn't. He had the whole thing figured out. All he had to do was cooperate with Warfield and *he* would be all right. Maybe even get a promotion.

Will was furious. But he was powerless to do a thing. There wasn't anything else to say.

"Made any decisions?" came a voice. It was the attractive woman from the reception desk, Rachel Clement. Only now she was standing by their table with an apron and a pad in hand, ready to take their order. It was something else to watch Hap switch gears from traitor to nice guy, Will thought as he watched Hap smile at her with all his charm, a big, unconvincing grin spreading across his face.

"Hey," Hap said, "you do everything round here?" He managed to slip in a lot of innuendo around the word *everything*. It was an ultimate Hap moment.

Just thinking about his family! Disgusted, Will downed his drink and stood from the table. "Lost my appetite," he told them, walking from the room.

SEVEN

Will's room was rustic with tongue-and-groove paneling and a wood floor covered with scatter rugs, but it wasn't exactly home away from home. He tossed his bag onto a king-size bed with a floral bedspread that could make a person dizzy if he stared at it too long. There was a TV set on a stand chained to the far wall, and a remote control attached to the bedside table to prevent it from being stolen. So much for the trusting nature of mankind.

Along with the TV, there were two armchairs, a small coffee table that looked as if it would collapse if you put your feet on it, matching table lamps with a kind of pottery base, a dresser, two drinking glasses in sanitary plastic, and a painting of an idealized Alaskan glacier on the wall. Every-

thing about the room was chintzy and touristy—
too many patterns, not enough space.

Will tried to think. There was nothing he could
do at the moment about Hap Eckhart, his unfaith-
ful partner. Or Warfield, the ambitious Internal Affairs prick in L.A. So Will propped up the half
photo of Kay Connell against the base of his bedside table lamp and tried to think about her. Her
smile still looked awkward and enigmatic, an unhappy teenage girl pretending to have a good
time.

Why? Will wondered. *What do you have to be unhappy about, Kay?* A good question to put to anyone, he supposed. Someone certainly could put
that question to him.

Will moved to the window. There was a great
view from his room, he had to concede: snowcapped mountains rising grandly in the distance,
bathed in the weird white glow that was neither
day nor night. Gloomily, he glanced at the digital
clock on the bedside table: 12:04 A.M.! How could
people live like this? Fortunately, there was a roller
blind on the window that he lowered into place.
Something was wrong with the spring and it took
him two tries to get the blind so that the lower end
came down all the way to the windowsill and
stayed there, blocking out the unnatural light.

At last, he had what he wanted—darkness!

Will undressed and got into bed, stretching out
beneath a thin blanket. He closed his eyes, imagin-

ing a dark night sky—the sky, for instance, the way it looked at night from the top of Mulholland Drive, with all of Los Angeles spread out twinkling below. But all Will could see, emblazoned on the inside of his eyelids, was light. White light. Even with the blinds down, he *knew* there was damn silver light shining outside the window! It bothered him in some subliminal way. It bothered him greatly.

Will glanced at the clock: 1:49 A.M. He turned over, from his right side to his left, certain the strategic move would put him to sleep. He was comfortable, drifting into a delicious presleep feeling. Like stepping onto a small boat and floating out from shore. He was falling, deeper and deeper . . .

Then, suddenly—

Rrrrrrrippppppp!

What the fuck was that? Will jerked upright in bed, staring at the window. The blind had just snapped open, rolling up upon itself, allowing in a flood of white light too bright to even look at without squinting.

"You've got to be kidding me!" Will cried.

But Alaska was not kidding. Not in the summer, when the sun never set, and an exhausted L.A. cop was trying to sleep.

Detective Ellie Burr never had any trouble sleeping. Eight hours every night, like clockwork, and she was fresh and eager to begin a new day. The summer mornings were especially wonderful to her. The clear Alaskan air was simultaneously crisp yet fragile, filling every corpuscle of her body with optimism and hope. Sometimes she just wanted to dance and sing, or maybe go jogging in the mountains, just for the sheer animal joy of being alive.

Ellie picked up Will and Hap at the Pioneer Lodge in the department Cherokee. Will slipped into the front, Hap into the back. She was glad for that. She admired Detective Will Dormer enormously and hoped to learn from him. Ellie believed in role models. She had loved watching Will yesterday, both in the morgue and at the Connell house, how he had used his *imagination* to reconstruct the life of the dead girl. Ellie was determined to soak up every crumb of advice and inspiration that she could.

At the moment, Will appeared to be weary. His face was gaunt and gray and pessimistic as he stared out the window at the passing streets. Ellie vowed to be more cynical herself. She knew she was too eager. A detective like Will Dormer had "seen it all"—she liked that phrase. Seen, by God, every sort of human depravity, vice, and corruption! Maybe one day she would be jaded, too. World-weary and wise.

As she drove, she tried to imagine what Will thought of Nightmute, staring at the town so solemnly out the window. It wasn't very impressive, she knew. Utilitarian industrial buildings, shops, and gas stations. But in the distance, the beautiful mountains!

"We can take the old highway," she suggested on a sudden impulse. "Show you a little more scenery. Or head straight over . . ."

She glanced at Will, then at Hap in the rearview mirror. They were both deep in thought. They hadn't even heard her.

"We'll head straight over," she concluded. They were driving to the high school to interview Randy Stetz, Kay's boyfriend. She wondered if Will was planning exactly how he was going to conduct the interview. Mapping out his strategy. She kept stealing looks at him. *He is so sad-looking!* It was very appealing, and somehow romantic. But there was something wrong with Detective Will Dormer this morning. She didn't know what it was, but it was more than simple sadness. He looked troubled. Like a man on the edge. The longer she studied him, the more she was certain that something was very wrong. And that troubled her, because she admired him so much.

What's wrong with Detective Will Dormer? she wondered.

But just then, to her embarrassment, he turned his shrewd eyes her way and caught her studying him. He smiled so subtly it was hard to say for certain it was any kind of smile at all.

"What kind of calls you get around here?" he asked.

"Oh, you know, drinking-related. Domestic abuse, bar fights. This time of year it's pretty quiet. There's work out on the boats, tourists in town. People here come from all over, come to live life the way they want to, so everybody keeps to themselves, you know. In winter, folks get a little edgy. All that dark. But the chief rarely lets me handle anything above a misdemeanor anyway."

She hadn't meant to let that last bit sneak out. Will's smile grew warmer, more sympathetic. "Don't give misdemeanors a bad rap," he told her.

Ellie sighed. "Small stuff. It gets boring."

"It's all about the small stuff," he assured her. "Small lies, small mistakes. People give themselves away in a misdemeanor same way they do in a murder case. It's all human nature."

Ellie listened intently, drinking in every word.

"Aren't you going to write that down?" he asked.

She started searching awkwardly in her pockets for a pad and pen, one hand on the wheel. Then she glanced over at Will and realized he was teasing her.

She grinned, good-natured. She didn't mind being teased by someone as smart and cool as Will Dormer. But she wouldn't make the same mistake again.

EIGHT

The high school was a sprawl of low buildings connected by covered walkways. Its institutional style was modern but without warmth or character of any kind. The parking lot was full of students' cars, mostly old pickup trucks and some ancient gas-guzzlers that rode low to the ground. There was a gymnasium with a curved roof at the far side of the parking lot, and a football field beyond that, bordered with bleachers.

Will wondered what it was like to attend high school in a town like Nightmute, Alaska. Did they have guns and gangs, as in L.A.? From the outside of the school, it looked to Will as if he had traveled in a time machine to the 1950s. But appearances weren't always accurate. In the *Ozzie and Harriet* fifties, pretty high school coeds like Kay Connell didn't end up naked and murdered, their bodies thrown onto the top of a trash heap.

Ellie led them to the administrative office, and from there a bald man with a bullet-shaped head took them to Randy's classroom. The bald man wore a short-sleeved white shirt and tie, but no coat. He was trim and neat and had a pocketful of pens, with a plastic pen protector to keep ink from getting on his shirt. Will imagined that the students made fun of him behind his back. He and Hap and Ellie waited in a hallway that smelled vaguely of ripe socks and old peanut butter and jelly sandwiches while the bald man slipped into the classroom.

Will watched through the glass window in the door as the man approached a teenage boy in the back row, bending over his desk. The boy was lanky, dressed in a grungy T-shirt and jeans. He looked like trouble. A face that was young, but far from boyish. Dingy, shoulder-length brown hair, muscular arms, suspicious eyes. Everything about his body language seemed to say, "What's in it for me?" The bald man whispered something into Randy's ear, and the teenager stood up with a sneer on his lips. The rest of the students began buzzing among themselves, a sea of whispers. This was true-life drama for them, probably a lot more interesting than whatever it was they were studying.

A girl with white-blond hair watched Randy

pass her desk. It was Tanya Francke, Kay's best friend, whose torn picture had ended up in Kay's wastepaper basket. In person, Tanya just missed being pretty, though she was certainly sexy in a coarse way. She broadcasted waves of eros and experience. The kind of girl who had grown up quickly, and whom teenage boys would be eager to get into the backseat of their cars. Her knowing eyes followed Randy's departure from the classroom until they came to Will, who was peering in at her from the glass. She held Will's gaze boldly, with a distinct sexual challenge, as though to say, "So what? You're an old fart, but I bet you want me, too, just like all the other guys."

Randy lumbered out of the classroom with the sneer still on his face, showing his dislike of authority. He was taller than Will, a loutish country boy with the scrawny yet wiry build of a grease monkey. They took him down the hall to an empty classroom. Randy slouched down into a desk, making himself at home.

Randy! What a name for a teenage boy! Will circled behind him.

"How are you coping, Randy?"

Randy was too bored to answer. Will moved around in front of him, and lowered his head to the boy's level.

"Doing okay, yeah?" Will turned to Hap. "He seems okay, doesn't he?"

"Got his grief under control," Hap agreed.

"Give me a chance, okay?" Randy blurted out angrily, deigning at last to speak. He flicked a look at the door. There were students peering in at him curiously as they passed. Randy didn't like that much. "You fuckers been *on* me since Monday."

"Friends making you nervous, Randy?" Will slipped into the desk beside the teenager, just so they could be side by side and friendly. "They think you did it? Killed her?"

The boy pulled out a cigarette from a pack in his jeans pocket. The cigarette was badly bent.

"No smoking on school premises," Hap told him.

"Sure thing, asshole."

Hap smiled at Will. "More Alaskan hospitality."

"Did you love her?" Will asked.

Randy lit his cigarette with elaborate unconcern, inhaling deeply.

Will started to repeat his question. "Randy, did you love—"

"Sure. She was nice."

Will looked up at Hap, who was standing with his arms folded, a look of amusement on his face. Randy concentrated on his cigarette.

"'She was nice,'" Will repeated to Hap. "Wow. That makes me all soft inside." He turned back to Randy. "Ever occur to you that she didn't love you back."

The teenager treated Will to a defiant stare. "She loved me. Wanted me every night."

"To pass the time. Girl like Kay's looking for more than some loser, right?"

Randy smiled. "What can I tell you, Officer? Love is blind. She loved me. I loved her. And no, I didn't kill her."

"You live on your own," Will mentioned, pausing significantly.

"Top of your grandpa's building," Hap added.

"No alibi for Friday night," Will pressed.

"Didn't know I was gonna need one," Randy said.

"At the party," Hap said, "what'd you fight about?"

"Stuff. I don't even remember. It was no big deal."

"People said it was a loud fight," Will told him.

"I guess," Randy allowed.

"Pretty rough."

"Wasn't rough."

"Not that time. Not like other times. Times she wouldn't listen. Times she didn't know when to shut up."

Randy's eyes flickered from Will to Hap, and back to Will again. "Keep fishing, man," he said. But his confidence was slipping.

"We saw the bruises, Randy," Hap said.

"They said she was beaten," the boy agreed.

"Not those bruises," Will told him. "Old bruises. *Your* bruises."

"Hey, I'm sick of this bullshit. I didn't do anything!"

"No?"

"No! So why don't you stop fucking with me and go find somebody who did it? See, you pricks think you—"

Will lost his patience. He grabbed the boy's shirt and moved closer, nose to nose.

"Listen to me. This fuck-the-world crap might work with your mama, might even work with local cops who've known you long enough to figure you're too *dumb* to have killed someone without a couple witnesses and a signed confession. But it doesn't work with me. We know things. We know you beat your girlfriend. And we know she was seeing somebody else. Somebody she might've gone to see after she walked out on you Friday night." Will let go of Randy's shirt, and paused significantly, letting his words work. "You gonna tell us who that somebody is, or are you so fucking stupid that you're gonna leave yourself as the last person who saw Kay alive?"

Randy blinked. He was starting to look sick, his face the pale gray color of a halibut's underside.

"I don't know," he said after a while.

"You don't know."

"I couldn't get her to tell me!"

Will ran his eyes over Randy's face, disgusted. He kept his voice quiet. "How hard did you try?"

Randy turned to Will with his last ounce of defiance. He smiled coldly. "Pretty hard," he admitted.

Will felt a rage of blood roar in his ears, an ocean of sound. He wanted to hit the kid so badly that for a moment he almost lost control. But Randy Stetz wasn't worth it, only a small-town loser who was living the best years of his life in high school, a time of blissful innocence compared to what would surely follow—the boredom and empty anger of a dead-end life.

Will rose with difficulty from the narrow school desk and chair, a unit that hadn't been designed with a middle-aged cop in mind. Leaving Randy Stetz to worry, he led the way out of the classroom into the hall, with Hap and Ellie behind him.

Hap spoke. "You don't think he . . ."

Will shook his head, dismissing the kid as a serious suspect. Hap nodded. As partners, they weren't getting on so great at the moment, but still they had worked together long enough so that their minds tracked in close tandem. Simply put, Randy Stetz was too stupid to be the perp of this particular murder. He might have beaten his girlfriend too hard, things could have gotten out of hand. But he would not have been smart enough to remove forensic traces of his crime, washing her hair and cutting her nails. The coldness of that act, the cunning . . . it would have required a more dangerous person.

Meanwhile, Ellie was watching him very

closely, her eyes wide with interest. He reached into his coat pocket, pulled out Kay's silver necklace, and handed it to her.

"Let's find out where this came from."

"Mrs. Connell doesn't know," Ellie told him. "And I checked with her friends, but they—"

"Try jewelry stores," Will interrupted.

"You think it's that important? We've got a lot of other—"

"The small things—remember? The second you're about to dismiss something, look at it again."

Ellie smiled, teasing. "You want me to write that down?"

Will smiled back, suddenly liking her more than he thought he might. They were about to leave the high school when Ellie's cell phone bleated. She put the device to her ear and Will could tell by her face that something important was going down.

NINE

Will burst into the bull pen, the common area of the police station. He was anxious, hoping that none of the local Sherlocks had managed to fuck up what appeared to be a major break. What he saw was not encouraging. A bunch of uniforms huddled around a desk. Too many people by far, a real circus, breathing and poking at the evidence, their backs to him.

"Where was it?" he demanded.

"In a fishing cabin on the beach," Fred Duggar answered, stepping back from the table.

Will could see it now. A patchwork knapsack resting on the desk. Or a daypack, whatever kids called them these days—in the interest of conformity, they all seemed to have them.

"Definitely Kay's?" He grabbed a pair of latex gloves from a utility shelf.

"Her books are in it," Chief Nyback said. The chief appeared pleased with himself.

"Couple of kids found it," said one of the uniformed cops, a lanky young man with a prominent Adam's apple. His name was Farrell, Will recalled.

"Cabin been secured?"

"Francis is headed there now," Fred said.

Will turned for confirmation to Chief Nyback, who understood the question in Will's eyes and nodded.

"Stop him," Will said. "Tell him to stay clear."

Nyback hesitated only a moment, then agreed. The chief picked up his cell phone to stop the officer in question while Will circled the knapsack like a vulture, slipping his hands into the latex gloves. Like most of Kay's belongings, the knapsack looked like something you could put together yourself, almost homemade. Will examined the two plastic clasps that held the bag closed, searching to see if there was anything unusual. Finally, very carefully, he opened the knapsack and pulled out two textbooks. The books were big and bright and optimistic, designed to snag the interest of high school students.

"Biology and algebra," he said. He turned to one of the uniforms. "Find out who she studied with."

After the books, he pulled out a small plastic

bag with *Hello Kitty*s all over it, very cute and feminine. He opened the zipper and dumped the contents of the bag onto the desk. There was makeup inside—lipstick and mascara—and several elastic hair bands. Will turned to Fred Duggar.

"Find out where she bought it."

Fred gave him a hard-ass look, letting it be known that he was not happy with makeup duty. Will could care less. He kept working at the blue knapsack, feeling a surge of excitement as he always did when there was a break in a case. He pulled out a well-worn paperback. It was a crime novel, which surprised him—from the idea he had of Kay, she would be more inclined, he thought, toward a Harlequin Romance. Maybe even poetry, something sentimental.

He examined the book and read the title aloud. *"Otherwise Engaged:* Another J. Brody Mystery." He looked up at the circle of cops watching him. "Who reads this kind of crap?"

Officer Farrell seemed offended. "I read that kind of crap."

Will pointed at the book. "Once it's dusted, read it," he told Farrell. "Anything strikes you, plotwise, underlined passages—*anything*, you let me know."

Next out of the patchwork knapsack came the best thing so far: a diary. It was smaller than the schoolbooks, but bigger than the paperback mystery. Imitation red leather with a brass clasp.

Something a teenage girl could pour her heart into. Will turned a few pages that were filled with neat, rounded handwriting. It was sad to see the earnest expressions of a young woman pondering her life, now that her life was over. Will closed the book and held it up to Ellie, looking her in the eye. "Every word!" he told her.

Ellie nodded, transfixed—at last, something interesting to do that wasn't a misdemeanor.

Will continued, pulling out a half-eaten sandwich and an apple core in a clear Ziploc bag. He held these prize items up to Fred. "Lab!" he ordered. He upended the pack, but there was nothing more inside. Santa Claus had finally run out of gifts. "That's it," he told the gathering.

Fred Duggar reached for the knapsack. "I'll put it into evidence."

"No," Will objected, stopping him.

Fred stiffened. He was a guy whose self-importance was easily affronted. "Why?" he demanded.

Will ignored him and turned to Ellie instead. "Call every radio and TV station from here to Anchorage. Tell them we're looking for the bag Kay Connell left the party with." Will checked his watch. "Get it on the air in the next hour."

At last, he turned back to Fred, holding up the knapsack. "Fill it with books," he said. "Put it back where it was found. It'll eat this guy alive, knowing he missed something this big."

A light seemed to come into Fred's eyes. He got it. A plan! Actual police *strategy*! He took the bag, excited now. Energy swept through the room as everybody saw exactly what Will had in mind, each of them heading off to accomplish their various duties.

Will was feeling pretty good, too, until he turned and found Hap looking at him, and the memory of all the mess in Los Angeles came flooding back. He might be in exile in far-off Alaska, but it was still not far enough from the Internal Affairs quagmire he had left behind. Will's mind started racing, imagining how things could turn bad. Suddenly, he wasn't at all sure of himself. It was a sneaky idea, using the knapsack to snare the killer. But it could backfire. For one, the media was not going to be pleased when they discovered they'd been lied to, and that could prove to be nasty. Lawsuits, even. It was a complicated world they inhabited. Nor was it inconceivable that some low-life defense attorney down the line would call Will's sneaky idea entrapment. If Will's reputation went down the toilet, if people were suspicious, if they didn't trust him anymore . . . these were the sorts of things that could happen in a blink of an eye. These were the sorts of things that ended careers.

Reluctantly, he walked over to Nyback and took the chief's arm. "Charlie, maybe this isn't such a hot idea. Just 'cause someone picks up that bag doesn't make him guilty."

Hap stepped closer, sensing trouble. "Will, it's solid!"

Will ignored his partner. "We should do this one by the numbers," he advised Charlie.

The chief was puzzled. He looked from Will to Hap, and back to Will again. At last, Will sighed and told Charlie the truth. "I.A.'s gonna be on my ass. I don't want this unraveling in court six months from now 'cause my rep's in the shit and they're pulling apart all my cases."

"That's bullshit, Will," Hap interrupted.

Will turned and looked at his partner, furious, sending daggers. "What the *fuck* do you care?"

The chief put a hand on Will's arm, calming him down. "Someone out there just beat a seventeen-year-old girl to death. Your job is to find him, Will. You're a cop, not a fucking lawyer." Charlie squeezed Will's arm. "Don't let I.A. cut your balls off."

"Charlie's right, Will," Hap threw in.

Will ignored Hap. He wouldn't lower himself to even look at his traitorous partner. It was a bad fix, and he didn't know what to think. But at last he nodded at Charlie. Whatever happened, they had to take the chance. There was a window of opportunity here to get the creep who had murdered Kay Connell.

It was a chance that might not come again.

TEN

Will studied the fishing cabin through binoculars from a hiding place behind a tangle of fallen trees on the beach about fifty yards away. The cabin where Kay Connell's knapsack had been found was old and obviously long abandoned by its owner, a wooden shack that couldn't have been more than ten feet by twelve, windowless. There was a single door and a roof of corrugated tin. Probably it served as a good place for low-rent lovers and teenagers intent to party.

Will lowered his binoculars and shifted his weight from one leg to another. They had been there several hours already, waiting for the killer to show. So far there was nothing, no one, but Will was patient. He had never minded being on a stakeout. It was relaxing in an odd way, like fishing.

Putting your bait in the water and waiting for a bite.

The cabin sat some distance from the ocean at the edge of a rocky gorge with a stream running through it. The beach was cold and damp and wild, a chaotic jumble of boulders piled up upon each other, with huge trees that had been washed ashore by storms, often resting on the boulders at crazy angles. It wasn't a spot where anyone would be tempted to put down a towel and go for a swim. They were less than a half hour's drive from town, but the shore there was primitive and lonely, like some primordial coast from the dawn of time. A fog was drifting in from the ocean, gathering around the jagged rocks. Will checked his watch. It was 7:23 in the evening, with no sign of sunset coming anytime soon—except for the fog, it might have been midafternoon. Weird, but for purposes of a stakeout Will had to agree that the prolonged day was welcome.

Hap and Farrell were nearby, crouching behind a boulder, comparing their guns.

"All plastic except for the barrel and firing pin," Farrell was saying. "Never rusts. What do you carry down in L.A.?"

"Smith and Wesson forty-five." There was macho pride in Hap's answer. A .45 wasn't some damn Yuppie gun, as Hap liked to point out to whoever would listen—for there was a fashion for cops in L.A. to carry increasingly fancy pieces. Not for Hap—just classic firepower that could blow a guy away.

"Excellent!" Farrell told him.

Will tuned them out. On the far side of the cabin, up above in the rocks, Fred Duggar was stationed with a uniformed cop named Rich, a tall, powerful-looking Inuit with his long raven hair pulled back in a ponytail. Closer at hand, Ellie appeared from around a rock with a thermos of coffee.

"Anything?" she offered.

Will shook his head.

"Maybe this guy doesn't listen to the radio," Farrell suggested.

"Prefers the voices in his head," Hap joked, putting on a spooky voice. Everyone except Will was getting bored; they would not have made jokes like this two hours ago. Hap took the thermos from Ellie and poured himself some coffee into a paper cup. "Will?" he said, holding the thermos over as a peace offering.

Will stared coldly at his partner, then turned away. If Hap cooperated with that I.A. fuck, Warfield, all the coffee in Alaska wasn't going to make amends between them. Will raised the binoculars once again to his eyes and studied the cabin. Nothing had changed except for the fog, which was rolling in more thickly, a blanket of ghostly white creeping up the rocky gorge, gathering around the wooden shack.

Will scanned up and down the rocky beach with his binoculars. At first he saw nothing. Then, yes—there was a figure, half lost in the fog, making its way across a small bridge that crossed the gorge toward the cabin. The fog made it impossible to tell anything about the person, even if it was a man or a woman. But someone had come to their party—that was the main thing. Now they needed to close in and take him.

Will's walkie-talkie sputtered to life. "I see someone!" It was Fred, from his position in the rocks. Hap and Farrell scrambled to their feet.

Will hissed into the radio. *"Fan out! Easy does it!"*

Slowly, very carefully, they moved closer over the rough terrain. With their guns drawn, Will and Hap came to the wooden bridge and began making their way across, while Farrell and Ellie climbed down into the gorge in order to approach the cabin from a different angle. From across the ravine, Will could just make out Fred and Rich scrambling over the boulders. Silently, inch by inch, they began closing in from their different directions. The figure, whoever it was, was about a dozen feet from the cabin now. Will thought they had him.

And then, just when everything was set, it all fell apart.

It was stupid. A single misstep. Will and Hap had crossed the bridge, while Farrell and Ellie had climbed up from the gorge to regroup. Will gestured down to Farrell to hand him the megaphone they had brought. Farrell was only a little ways below him; it shouldn't have been a problem. But Farrell was balanced badly on a log. He reached up to hand the megaphone to Will, then slipped. Staggering to regain his balance, he accidentally keyed the megaphone. There was a screech of feedback, an electronic scream that pierced the evening. Up ahead, the figure in the fog looked about wildly, then started running, racing toward the cabin.

"Go! Go! Go!" Will shouted, disgusted. Everyone jumped into action. Fred and Rich, Will and Hap, Ellie and Farrell—all of them scrambling over the rough terrain as fast as they could toward the shack. The killer got there first, disappearing inside, slamming the door behind him. *A dumb move!* He was trapped inside! Will felt a surge of relief. They were going to get him after all.

Fred and Farrell came sliding down a gravel slope in front of the cabin door, just as Will arrived.

"Police!" Will called inside, pointing his .45 at the door.

There was no answer. Will stepped back, raised his right foot, and kicked the door in. The wood, half rotten, smashed into splinters. He rushed inside in a low crouch, moving his pistol side to side . . . but the shack was empty! There was no one. Only some old fishing nets and a wooden table.

Will moved forward, alert for the slightest

sound. The guy couldn't simply vanish. He turned about slowly, and soon saw the explanation: a crack in the floor at the far corner of the room, a trapdoor. Will rushed over, flung the trapdoor open, and thrust his gun down into the opening. There was nothing but darkness. The killer was gone.

"Fuck!" he cried. He motioned urgently to the others. "Down to the water. Spread out! Go!"

They took off, leaving Will alone in the cabin. He took a deep breath, then jumped into the darkness below. It was a leap of faith or desperation—he wasn't sure.

Splash!

He came down into a foot of standing water, nearly losing his balance. He staggered and did a little dance, hitting his shoulder hard against a rock wall. Wherever he was, the place was hellish. There were strange echoes in the dark. Water dripping somewhere in a closed space, a stereophonic *plip, plip, plip*. A distant rumble of surf. The darkness seemed to be breathing, as if he were inside a lung.

Will realized that he was in a tunnel of some kind and that there had to be an exit. If the killer had managed to escape this way, he could, too. He moved forward along slippery rocks, slowly at first, wading through the standing water, feeling for the walls with his hands. There was a dank, fishy smell in the air. It was an unclean odor he didn't want to think about. Rigid with tension, he kept moving. Before long, he noticed a dim circle of light up ahead, at the end of the tunnel. He began to move more quickly, gathering speed. The rocky walls lightened around him. He tripped and splashed, sprinting now, anxious to get free of this nightmarish place. At last, the echoes receded and he came out into the open.

Only, it *wasn't* open. Will found himself in an enclosed white blanket of fog—blinding white after the darkness of the tunnel. The fog was so thick he could barely see the gun in his hand in front of him. He stopped, breathing hard, and tried to get his bearings. There were indistinct sounds all around him. The surf? Footsteps? *Someone breathing?* He wasn't sure of anything. It was like being lost in a dream.

He clutched his gun and moved forward, feeling his way over the jagged rocks that littered the beach. He stumbled, hearing something ahead, banging his knee. The fog opened and closed around him, drifting, showing occasional patches of the land ahead. He jumped from the rock he was on onto a bigger, flat-sided slab that was slick with mist. He made his way up onto a ridge, scrambling over a huge boulder. There was the sound of water ahead. He stopped abruptly, his foot moving out into empty space. He stepped back, just in time.

Below him there was a long drop, more than twenty feet straight down into a running stream.

He heard footsteps behind him. Will spun around, ready to fire. A ghostly figure emerged from the mist. It was Officer Farrell, and he looked scared.

"Dormer!" he cried, relieved to find another human being.

Suddenly, Will saw something behind Farrell. A movement. A dark figure, farther back on the rocks, heading their way. Will raised his gun arm and took aim.

"Who's there?" he called.

There was no answer. The figure disappeared, swallowed in the drifting fog. Keeping his finger on the trigger, Will waited for the fog to clear. It had to be the killer. Anyone else would have returned his call.

Every sense in Will's body was alert to danger.

There he was! The mist shifted, showing a hint of human form.

A shot rang out. *Bang!* It was the figure in the mist, firing at them. Will dropped down into a crouch. He was okay, but he saw Farrell whip around and fall onto the rocks with a cry of outrage. Will scrambled toward him. Farrell lay clutching his leg in pain, blood flowing between his fingers.

"Okay!" he gasped. "I'm okay."

Will peered upward at the rocks, looking hard

into the fog for any sign of the figure with the gun. There was no time to worry about Farrell. He saw a form against the whiteness, a person trying to get away. Then the fog closed behind him, like a curtain pulling shut. Will hurried after where the figure had disappeared, plunging forward from rock to rock. He kept going, clumsily moving down the beach, trying his best to see.

He didn't seem to be getting anywhere. The fog was impenetrable. Will could be going around in circles for all he knew. The killer had the advantage. He knew the lay of the land here and could very well be long gone. Will stopped, listening intently. But all he heard was his own rapid breathing, sharp in his chest. Then he heard something else. A splashing not far ahead, the sound of feet moving through shallows.

Will continued more slowly, his gun ready. He could hear the splashing more closely at hand. He was gaining. He came around a boulder, and there he was . . . a silhouette in the fog, arm extended, holding a gun. Will dropped to one knee, aimed, and pulled the trigger. But there was no report, only a dry click. His gun was jammed!

Will had a backup. In one fluid motion, he tossed his .45, reached behind his back for his 9mm in a holster on his belt, pulled out the gun, sighted on the silhouette . . . and fired. There was an explosive boom, strangely muffled in the fog. The figure on the rock stumbled and dropped. Will

waited, tense and alert. There was silence, no re-
turning fire, but on this strange evening where
everything had gone wrong, he didn't trust anything to luck.

At last, he crawled forward. Something caught
his eye. It was an old .38 Smith & Wesson lying on
the rocks, about to be swept away by rushing
water from a small creek that was running to the
sea. Keeping his eye on the figure ahead, Will
reached down with one hand, grabbed the gun by
its barrel, and dropped it into his coat pocket.

A dozen feet away, the figure was trying to
crawl away on his stomach, making a scraping
sound against the rock. He was badly hurt, groaning with pain, but possibly still dangerous. Will
approached warily, keeping his gun on the killer's
back. It was a man, dressed in a suit. He was trying in vain to get away, but going nowhere, like
some beached sea creature gasping out its last
breath. Will froze. The scraping sound he'd heard
was a gun, a big .45 in the man's hand that was
slapping against the rock. Will kicked the gun
away. Finally, he grabbed the man violently by his
shoulders and rolled him over.

It took Will a second for his brain to register
what his eyes were trying to tell him:

It . . . was . . . *Hap!*

Will crashed to his knees. He holstered his
backup piece and took hold of his partner with
both hands. But Hap tried to push him away.

There was blood drooling from his mouth and his eyes were full of accusation. He was trying to roll over, get away from Will.

"You . . . you shot . . ." Hap's voice was barely more than a whisper.

"Don't try to talk," Will told him.

"Get away from me!" He made an effort to squirm from Will's embrace.

Will stared at Hap, trying to explain. "No! Hap . . . I couldn't . . . *I couldn't see.* . . ."

But there was dumb fear in Hap's eyes. He arched his back and looked wildly into the fog over Will's shoulder, searching for help.

"Help!" His voice was a dying hiss, barely audible. *"Somebody!"*

Will could only shake his head, dumbfounded. "No, no, Hap! Listen to me! Hap!"

But it was no good. Hap was dying before his eyes, fading fast. Will ripped off his tie and tried to find the wound. There was warm blood pumping out of a soggy place in Hap's shirt, the right side of his chest. Hopelessly, Will pressed his tie against the wound, trying to keep the fragility of life from slipping away.

Will raised his head and shouted desperately into the fog, "Man down! We got a man down here!"

But when he looked again, Hap was more than down. He was dead. Motionless. His eyes were open, still staring at Will with an infinity of accusation. *You killed me, partner!*

Will couldn't absorb the enormity of what he had done. He heard voices in the fog, footsteps approaching, splashing, people calling to one another. It was chaos. Fred Duggar was the first to emerge, gun drawn. He took in the scene, his eyes full of shock.

"Which way?" Fred demanded.

Will was beyond comprehension. He held on to Hap's body, lost, looking up at Fred without recognition.

"Dormer!" Fred shouted. "Which way'd he go?"

Will didn't know. He was confused and scared. He gazed off meaninglessly to the right, staring into the blinding fog. Fred seemed to take that as a sign, a cue for action. He dashed off in that direction. But it was hopeless. For Will, there was nothing that could make this right.

Ellie stepped out of the mist and looked down at him with concern. Will hardly registered her presence. He cradled Hap in his arms, seeing nothing except the lingering accusation that was frozen in the dead man's eyes.

You killed me, partner!

ELEVEN

Later that night, Will sat in Chief Charlie Nyback's office with the door closed, just the two of them. Charlie wanted an explanation. Will was a mess. Hap's blood was still all over his shirt. Wet and disheveled, he felt about as bad as he had ever felt in his life.

Charlie was sympathetic, but he was trying to get it right.

"So Farrell went down. You gave chase, and after you left Farrell, you heard the killer's second shot. Then you ran down to the water and found Hap?"

Will could only stare dumbly straight ahead. His mind felt as if it were in a locked box.

"Will? Is that what happened?" Charlie asked gently.

Will looked up. He could still tell the truth: *It was foggy, I couldn't see. I shot my partner by mistake.* But was that really the truth? And with the I.A. mess in L.A. and Hap set to testify against him, who would believe it? *Hap* hadn't believed it! Meanwhile, there was Charlie offering an easy way out. All Will had to say was that he had left Farrell wounded, he had made his way down to the water's edge, and he had found Hap already dead. Charlie was watching him intently. Slowly, Will nodded. He took the plunge into falsehood. *Yes, that's the way it was. Or ought to have been.*

Charlie sighed. "Was Hap still—"

But Will couldn't tolerate any more cross-examination. He jumped to his feet like a wild man and swiped his hand across Nyback's desk, bringing everything crashing to the floor. Books, papers, a coffee cup, a telephone directory, a framed photograph—everything scattering before the force of his anger.

"Why didn't I know about that goddamn tunnel?" Will cried. He began pacing up and down the office, nearly crazy. Charlie leaned back in his chair and watched patiently.

"You don't move in on an armed suspect without knowing his exits!" Will shouted, still not spent.

"There's a bunch of those tunnels out there," the chief told him calmly. "From mines closed sixty years ago. I don't even know most of them myself, and I grew up here." Charlie crouched over and began picking up things from the floor. He was a good man, solid gold, which only made Will feel worse.

"I *had* him, Charlie. Close as you are now. I could *smell* the son of a bitch, and I blew it."

"There's no point blaming yourself—"

"I fucked everything up."

Charlie fixed him with a look that was steady as a mountain. "Don't you come apart on me, understand? I need *you* to find this bastard."

Will was speechless. Even now it wasn't too late to tell the good man the truth. As he paced the floor, his very soul torn in half, there came a soft knocking on the door. Ellie Burr stepped in. She didn't seem to know where to look. Nyback rose to greet her.

"You wanted to see me?" she asked.

"You're on Detective Eckhart's shooting," the chief told her.

Ellie was confused. "We know what happened. I'm on the Connell case. . . ."

"Anchorage wants to send someone up. I said we could handle it ourselves. We can, can't we?"

Ellie glanced at Will, and then back to Nyback. Her eyes were filled with grief. "Sure," she said.

"Write it up. Doesn't have to be Shakespeare. Just enough to fry the bastard a couple minutes longer. Right, Will?"

Will came back from a long ways away. He

watched Ellie nod and back out of the office. "I'm gonna check the roadblocks," he told the chief suddenly.

"You're gonna take a breather," Charlie insisted.

"I need to find this guy—"

"You need *sleep*. But first . . ." Nyback sighed and looked away. "First you have to call Trish Eckhart."

Charlie stepped out of the office, giving Will some privacy. Will sat at the chief's desk, staring at the black telephone, working up the nerve to make the call to Hap's wife.

What in God's name was he going to say to her? More lies, because he sure as hell couldn't tell her the truth! That was the worst of it: the unclean feeling he had. Will Dormer understood he had crossed a threshold and from now on his life was going to be full of lies, big and small.

At last, he picked up the phone and dialed the familiar number of Hap's home in the San Fernando Valley. It was a home where Will had gone for many dinners and backyard barbecues. A child answered. It was Hap's little girl, Jenny.

"Jenny, it's Will," he told her in a careful voice. "Can you put your mother on?"

He listened as the little girl went running through the house. "Mommy, Mommy—it's Wi-i-ill!" she called. The wait for Trish to come onto the phone was unbearable. Will's mouth was dry and there was a taste of ash on his tongue.

Suddenly, she was on the phone, so clear she could have been in the next room. "Yes?" Her voice was tense, because a late-night telephone call was a cop's wife's worst fear.

"Trish? It's Will."

"What happened?" she exploded. "They won't tell me—"

"It's Hap," he told her.

They were both silent, awkwardly. Then they both tried to speak at once.

"Is he okay?"

"Hap's dead. He's dead, Trish."

There was more silence on the California end. Will shifted the phone and closed his eyes. "Trish?"

"How can that be?" she demanded, her voice breaking.

Will tried to explain. "We were chasing this guy. . . . Hap got shot. . . . Trish, I can't tell you how sorry—"

She was sobbing. Her words came out in a tumble of emotion. "What was he doing, Will?"

"We were . . . this guy killed a girl. We found him, cornered him. He ran. . . . Hap . . ." Will couldn't go on. The lie, the awfulness of it was too much. "I'm so sorry," he managed.

"Did he suffer?"

Will shifted uncomfortably in Chief Nyback's swivel chair. "No, I don't—"

"Did he *say* anything?"

Will closed his eyes, remembering. "When I found him . . ." Will breathed, full of the memory of Hap's accusing eyes, wishing the truth away. "When I found him . . . he was peaceful."

Trish didn't speak for a moment. Will wondered if she believed him, if he would need to lie some more. When she spoke again, her voice was very quiet, as though something in her had died.

"Did you get him? The . . . the—"

"No," he admitted, flushing with shame.

"You *find* him." Trish was angry now. Grief counselors said that was a good thing. "You find him. And when you do . . . you don't arrest him!"

Will listened, staring at the far wall.

"You understand me, Will Dormer? Don't you dare fucking arrest him! *Understand?*"

Will swallowed hard. He wanted to say something to her. He didn't know what. Something soothing. Something that would lay this whole matter to rest.

"Trish, listen to me. . . ."

But he had lost her. The connection was broken. Trish had hung up. Will put down the phone carefully, as if it were made of glass. Then he looked up and saw Ellie Burr studying him through the glass door of the office. He couldn't imagine what she might be thinking.

It didn't matter. Nothing mattered anymore. He stood up abruptly, crossed the room, flung open the door, and asked Ellie for the keys to the Jeep Cherokee. He didn't know where he wanted to go. Anywhere else would do.

TWELVE

Will drove like a maniac from the police station, tearing around a corner in the Cherokee, his knuckles white on the wheel. The streets were empty and speed was the next best thing to screaming.

He pulled over to the curb, sick to his stomach, and staggered into a narrow alley between two buildings. There was a Dumpster that smelled terrible, like rotting flesh. Will leaned against a wall and vomited. He stayed there awhile, propped against the wall, saliva dripping from his mouth.

He didn't think it could get any worse than that. But then he looked down and found the source of the rotting smell. It was a dead dog, eyes staring, fur matted, its teeth bared by decay. Horrible!

Will reeled away, pursued by demons. All of them shouting in his head: *Liar! Liar! Liar!*

Ten minutes later Will walked into the glass-and-stone lobby of the Pioneer Lodge. The desk was deserted and there was no one around. He could hear a radio from a back room behind the reception area. A male voice was reading the news:

"... *earlier this evening in an abortive attempt to apprehend a suspect in the murder of seventeen-year-old local resident Kay Connell. He was forty-five ...*"

The radio clicked off, midsentence, for which Will was grateful. He didn't want to hear it all again. Rachel Clement, the attractive receptionist/waitress, appeared from the back room. She stopped in her tracks when she saw Will, taking in the bloodstains on his shirt. After the first moment of shock, her eyes filled with kindness.

"I'm sorry," she told him softly.

Will nodded, unable to speak.

"It's been on the news for hours. We're not used to this sort of thing." She reached for his key on a hook behind her. When she turned back, she paused, remembering. "He was standing right there. Just last night." She shook her head, a good woman trying to absorb a bad thing. "Was I nice to him?"

Will took the key from her hand. "He liked you," he said. It wasn't much, but she was obviously upset and he wanted to give her something.

He made his way along the outside walkway to his room. It was close to midnight but the sky overhead was white with unnatural twilight lighting up the snowcapped mountains behind the town. Exhausted, Will closed the door behind him, glad to be alone. The first thing he did was pull down the blind, shutting out the terrible light from the midnight sky. Tonight he didn't plan to take any chances on the blind rolling up unexpectedly. He flicked on the overhead light and searched about the room for something heavy. There was a decorative vase on the bureau he thought would do. He lowered the blind another half inch to create some overlap, then used the vase to weigh it down in place against the windowsill. The balance was a little tricky, but he felt better knowing that the blind would stay put.

Will was about to toss his coat onto a chair when he remembered the gun he had found earlier on the rocks. He had forgotten about the pistol, a complicating factor. He pulled the weapon out from the coat and weighed it in his hand. It was a snub-nosed Smith & Wesson .38 revolver, one of the most popular handguns ever made. There must be a zillion of them in peace-loving America. Will sniffed the barrel. One shell had been fired and there was a lingering scent of gunpowder.

It was almost certainly the killer's gun, and this created a problem for Will. If he was right, bullets from the gun would match the slug that had

wounded Farrell, but not the one that had killed
Hap Eckhart. Will sat on the edge of the bed, holding the revolver. Unfortunately, that was the difficulty with lies. Once you began, you couldn't stop.
If you didn't watch it, the lies got more and more
complicated, until they collapsed under their own
weight. Yet this situation in itself wasn't so difficult. Will was an expert in such things. All he had
to do was make the .38 Smith & Wesson disappear.

The floor of his room was polished wood planks
with colorful scatter rugs over it, Alaskan rustic.
This gave him an idea. He began walking slowly
up and down the room, testing the floorboards. It
took a few moments but at last he found what he
was after, a squeak. Will had a Swiss Army knife in
his bag and for the next half hour he worked on
the board, prying it loose. The work was satisfy-
ing, something concrete to wrap his mind around.
He managed to pull up a three-foot section of
floorboard. Very carefully, he used his handker-
chief to wipe the gun clean of his prints; then he
slipped the .38 down into the joists and put the
board back into place. When he was finished, the
floor appeared just as it had earlier, undisturbed.

Will felt better than he had felt for a number of
hours. He was taking matters into his own hands,
getting somewhere. Then he walked into the bathroom and caught sight of himself in the mirror. *The
blood on his shirt!* It was more than a stain—it was
an accusation. Will slipped off the shirt and didn't

feel good anymore. He filled up the washbasin with warm water, opened one of the little motel soap bars, and began working on the stain, scrubbing at the fabric with quiet desperation.

He wondered if his life would ever feel clean again.

He couldn't sleep. He lay in bed hopelessly turning from one side to another. He played games with himself, telling himself it didn't matter. Trying not to look at the digital clock on the bedside table. Then finally looking, to see it was 3:58 A.M. The colon blinked maddeningly at him, counting off the passing seconds.

In a single furious motion, Will swept the clock off the table into the drawer and slammed it shut.

But still he couldn't sleep!

It was intolerable just lying there, the wheels of his mind turning like a clock. Minute after minute, hour after hour. He stared at the window, at the light leaking in from the edge of the blind. The light seemed to grow stronger, seeping farther along the wall, bleeding into the room, like a spreading stain.

Will turned away. But now what? For a second he thought he saw a girl standing by his bedside table, staring down at him. Kay Connell! She was one more regret to add to all his other regrets. A murdered girl whose killer he had allowed to go free tonight. Violently, Will turned over in bed and shut his eyes. He was determined to tune out his anguish and escape to a world of blissful darkness and sleep.

But sleep would not come. For the second night, insomnia gripped him in its talons.

In the morning, Will Dormer found an espresso stand down the road from his motel. He stood at the counter, staring at a large cup of black coffee, the steam circling into the air. He had no stomach for anything more solid than coffee. His eyes were bloodshot. He felt unreal, as if he were dreaming awake. Two Inuit children stood near the counter, studying him with huge brown eyes.

Were they accusing him, too?

He turned away. His eyes came to a newspaper on the counter. *The Nightmute Ledger.* The headline read: L.A. COP KILLED BY CONNELL SUSPECT.

Will downed the scalding coffee. The bitterness turned over in his stomach like a car engine trying to start. He told himself he was okay. He didn't need sleep. He would nail the fuck who had killed Kay Connell. He would get through this. Everything . . . would . . . be . . . okay!

But first he needed to cover all his bases, and make certain his lie was solid.

THIRTEEN

St. Francis Hospital was a busy place, a sprawling one-story modern building that looked as though it had been designed by the same architect who had made the high school. Everything was as cheerful as the budget had allowed, full of bustle and motion and bright plastic colors.

Will found Officer Farrell in a private room that was, by his figuring, almost directly above the basement morgue. Probably the hospital didn't advertise that fact. Farrell was in bed reading the paperback novel found in Kay's knapsack: *Otherwise Engaged:* Another J. Brody Mystery. Will tossed a Snickers bar onto the wounded man's lap. Farrell looked up, his face brightening.

"Didn't take you for the hospital-visiting type."

"I'm not." Will studied the wounded leg. "Clean through, huh?"

Farrell nodded. "No souvenir. Bullet got lost in the rocks."

Will felt a surge of optimism. That was good news. But he kept his expression neutral. "There's always next time," he said.

Farrell smiled and shook his head. Will sat on a chair for visitors by the bed.

"Ever been shot, Detective Dormer?"

"Yeah," Will answered distantly. "Kinda itches, don't it?"

Farrell grinned. He was a good-natured guy. But his grin saddened as he studied Will. "I'm sorry about Detective Eckhart."

Will nodded. He watched as Farrell struggled to find the right words.

"And . . . I'm sorry about that megaphone. Maybe if I hadn't . . . maybe things would've been different."

Will leaned forward. "Farrell. Let me tell you something. None of us is perfect. We do our best is all. We weren't out there running around in that fog for our health, were we?"

Farrell shook his head. But he wasn't convinced.

"Anything that happened out on that beach is the fault of one man and one man alone—the man who beat Kay Connell to death. You got that?"

Will had spoken with more force than he had intended. *Am I trying to convince myself?* The words worked on Farrell, at least. Will watched the young cop think about what he had said, then brighten.

"Thanks," Farrell told him.

"And now we gotta catch him." Will rose to his feet, hesitating before asking the next question. "Did you get a look at him?"

"When?"

"After I left you. Did you see anything?"

Farrell sighed. "I wasn't looking, to be honest. I was in a whole lot of pain. And when I heard that second shot, I kept my goddamn head down. Sorry."

Will stared at him, wondering if Farrell was telling all that he knew. Will felt a surge of paranoia that maybe Farrell had already passed on a different story to Chief Nyback . . . but that was crazy. He was worrying over nothing. Officer Farrell had a wide-open face, easier to read than a book. Will relaxed. The man had seen nothing. It was what Will had come to St. Francis Hospital this morning hoping to hear.

"No, no. Don't be sorry," he told the wounded cop.

Later that morning, Will sat near the window in the bull pen at the Nightmute police station, listening to Chief Nyback address the gathered department. It was a combination pep talk and discussion of the case. The room was crowded.

Every cop in the department, on-duty and off-, was in attendance.

Will's mind wandered. There were so many small details that came up in an investigation, unforeseen things you couldn't control. Details that could haunt a person with a secret to hide. He brought his attention back to what Nyback was saying. He needed to concentrate, pay attention.

". . . Nightmute hasn't lost an officer in thirty-seven years. Hap Eckhart wasn't from here, but he was one of us on this case. A fine detective and an even better man." He turned at last to Will. "Anything you'd like to add, Will?"

Will felt every eye in the room upon him. His stomach was queasy from the bitter coffee he'd been drinking. He forced himself to shake his head, casually.

"All right, then," the chief said briskly. The pep talk was over. "Let's get to it!"

Chairs scraped and there was a shuffling of feet as the Nightmute PD got to it, rising with determination. Will was grabbing his coat when he saw Ellie Burr coming his way. He turned and tried to ignore her—she was the last person he wanted to see, so eager and full of admiration. But there was no possibility of escape.

"Detective?"

He turned and faced her. Ellie had a map in her hand that she obviously wanted to show him.

"I'm sorry, but I was asked to write the report

on . . ." She sighed and lowered her eyes. "You know what I was asked to write the report on." She raised her eyes more boldly. This was clearly hard for her. "Could you . . . point out where you were when you heard the second shot?"

Will took the map from her. The beach was marked out. The cabin, the stream, the tunnel. There were several red circles to show where Farrell had been shot, and where Hap had died. Will felt a sinking feeling just to see a diagram of this place, and remember all over again.

Ellie observed his distress, and she was apologetic. "I'm sorry to have to—"

"You're doing your job, Ellie." He pointed to a spot on the map, close to where Farrell had been wounded. "I was about here." He handed her back the map and smiled, just to show that he was a good sport about her questions. "No sign of Farrell's bullet, then?"

Ellie shook her head. "But we'll have the other one for ballistics after the . . . after the autopsy," she managed.

Will turned away. One lie led to another; it never ended. He wondered if he was going to need to get rid of his 9mm automatic, his backup. That would be a pity, because he had always thought of it as his lucky gun . . . until now.

FOURTEEN

The rocky beach with the fishing cabin looked very different today, clear of fog, windswept, and starkly beautiful. Gulls floated in the currents overhead, screeching their lonely cries to the waves. Facing east, you could see the wooded foothills rising from the beach in a long graceful curve to the jagged snowcapped peaks beyond. To the west, the ocean was hard blue and cold, melting into the horizon.

Detective Ellie Burr wished it had been as clear as this last night. Everything would have happened differently. Chances were Hap Eckhart would still be alive, and maybe they would have gotten the creep who had killed poor Kay Connell. Meanwhile, Ellie was not thrilled to have the job of writing up the report on Hap's death. It seemed to her a matter that any officer could have done. Once again Chief Nyback refused to give her the chance she wanted to be a *real* detective. Nevertheless, she was determined to write up the best report that anyone had ever written on an open-and-shut case. When you were twenty-three years old and a woman, you had to work twice as hard as everybody else just to stay in place.

Ellie had brought three uniformed officers with her to help gather all the necessary measurements. She outranked them all, but still, they were guys and it was difficult as hell to get any respect from them.

She walked from the cabin toward the shore, carrying the map and talking into a small tape recorder. Rich, who had been involved in part of the operation last night, followed after her with a camera, taking pictures.

Ellie spoke in a deeper voice, hoping this would make her sound more professional on tape. ". . . at this point, Detective Dormer encountered Officer Farrell Brooks. The suspect, obscured by fog, shot Officer Brooks in the *vastus externus* of the upper left thigh. . . ."

As she talked into the machine, they arrived at the spot where Farrell had been shot. Francis, one of the uniformed officers, was hanging out near the rock where Farrell had fallen. He was smoking and looked bored.

"Okay, Francis, you're Farrell," she told him.

He nodded. But he didn't get it. He just stood there sucking on his cigarette.

"You've been *shot*," she explained.

He got it now. She wanted him to lie down and do some acting. *Reconstruction of the crime scene* was how her teacher at the academy had put it. Francis gave her an exasperated look. "C'mon, Ellie!" he complained. They had known each other since high school. She had briefly dated his younger brother. But she gave him a look right back, knowing that if Francis refused to do what she told him, she might as well turn in her gold shield right now.

With a sigh and looking very put out, Francis started to lower himself onto the ground. He stopped in midmotion, frowning at a dark patch on the rocks.

"Is this his *blood*?"

Ellie wondered how Will would handle such a situation. *Make a joke*, she decided. "Ketchup, maybe," she told him. "Was he eating a hot dog?"

Ellie grinned, pleased with herself, and hopped lightly onto the next rock.

She kept moving, surveying the crime scene, studying the map, then looking at the rocky beach, then back at the map again. Trying to put everything together in her mind, how it had all happened.

She felt something was wrong, but didn't know

what it was. Maybe it was only her inexperience, but something nagged at her. She crossed a little stream near the waterline, speaking into the tape recorder in her deeper-than-normal detective voice:

"Detective Dormer gave chase, losing the suspect in the fog. Dormer then heard a second shot from a northeasterly direction. . . ."

Up ahead, another officer was lying on the rock where Hap Eckhart had died. Only it was high tide now and he was in several inches of seawater that ebbed and flowed around him. Ellie frowned. None of these guys understood the importance of getting the crime reconstruction *absolutely* right in every detail.

"He wasn't lying that way," she said moodily.

"How do you know?" It was Rich, coming up beside her.

"'Cause I saw him."

Ellie walked over to the cop who was lying in the water. "Move around to your left," she told him.

He was shivering. "We about done? I'm freezing my nads off, here."

Ellie stepped back as the officer repositioned himself. This was looking better, more the way Hap had been. And yet . . . what was it that was nagging her?

She was thinking hard, wondering, when Francis called to her from higher up on the beach, standing near the rock where Farrell had been wounded.

"Ellie!" he shouted. "Think I found something!"

She turned and saw he was holding some small object raised high in his hand. When she walked over, she saw it was a bullet slug.

Ellie grinned, suddenly happy, in love with all the world. This was an important find, and she couldn't help but think about Will Dormer, and how impressed he was going to be when he heard the good news.

While Ellie was on the beach, Will Dormer was a few minutes away on a dirt road above the beach that led to the fishing cabin in the woods. A line of volunteers, all townspeople, were stretched out through the trees, inching their way forward through the woods, their heads down. Will and Fred Duggar walked behind them, keeping a sharp eye for anything the searchers might have missed.

"Anything he might've dropped or stepped on, you put in a bag!" Will called to the line of moving people. He had told them this already, but with volunteers you had to be persistent. "Cigarette butts, gum wrappers, coins—a suspect often leaves something behind."

Fred seemed skeptical. "They should start farther back," he said, gesturing up to the forest on the east side of the road.

Will shook his head. "Waste of time. He stayed down by the water as far as he could." Will gazed down the slope of the hill at the fishing shack and the beach beyond. He could see Ellie in the distance walking about with a group of Nightmute's finest. "I saw him over those rocks—he knew he'd lose us down there."

Fred shrugged. He seemed about to say something sarcastic when his cell phone began to bleep.

"Duggar," he answered, holding the black plastic phone to his ear. He listened for a moment, then grinned. "How'd he find it?" he said into the phone.

Will froze. He had just noticed a man, one of the searchers, near the end of the line. His back was to Will, but everything about him was familiar—the way he moved, the shape of his shoulders.

For chrissake, it's Hap!

Will couldn't breathe. He didn't know whether to go over and put his arms around his partner and laugh with relief. Or run.

"Dormer?" Fred was saying, trying to get his attention.

Just then, the man at the end of the line turned. Will could see him better now. *No, it isn't Hap.* Only an eerie resemblance. Will found he could breathe again. He turned to Fred.

"They found Farrell's bullet. Looks like a thirty-eight," Fred told him.

Will nodded. *Fuck!* It wasn't easy to keep his expression neutral when all his luck was going sour. His mind raced. A .38 slug! It had to be from the Smith & Wesson he had hidden underneath the floorboards in his room.

"After the autopsy, we'll get both bullets to the lab in Anchorage, get a fix on the murder weapon," Fred announced, strutting with pride.

Will nodded, sick to his stomach.

Fred's grin had an edge to it, sharp enough to cut sheet metal. "That is, if it's all right with you," he added sarcastically.

Will turned back to the beach below, watching Ellie and her crew finishing up. He had already had the glimmering idea of how he might save himself. But he was starting to wonder if this nightmare would ever end.

FIFTEEN

Rachel Clement was working behind the reception desk at the Pioneer Lodge when Will came in that evening, dog-tired, dragging his steps. She looked up at him and smiled. It was a simple smile, but warm and human. A smile to melt the glacier in any man's heart.

Another time, another place, Will thought moodily. Unfortunately, this was not the time, nor the place.

"Guy came to see you earlier," she said, handing him his key. "Said he was your new partner."

Will frowned. "Fred Duggar?"

"Didn't leave a name. Said you were expecting him."

New partner? It didn't compute. Fred was the only person who came close to fitting the bill, but he couldn't imagine Fred describing himself that way. Besides, he wasn't expecting Fred. Will felt a vague unease. Meanwhile, he spotted a roll of transparent tape on Rachel's desk. He reached for it.

"Can I?"

Sure, she told him, picking up the ringing telephone. "Pioneer Lodge . . . hold on a second." Rachel covered the receiver with her hand and glanced at Will. "John Warfield," she said. "He's called a couple of times."

Will sighed. Warfield, the Internal Affairs jerk in Los Angeles, was the last person on the planet he wanted to talk with at the moment.

"Want me to lie?" Rachel asked, reading his face.

He shook his head. Unfortunately, Warfield wasn't going away. Will took the phone. "Dormer," he said into the receiver, without joy.

"I've been trying to reach you, Detective. I'm sorry about your partner. Must be a shock."

John Warfield had a smooth voice, well modulated, almost like an announcer on some slick FM station. It was a voice that was going places. A voice built for success. Will said nothing.

"Least *I* was pretty shocked," Warfield went on, undeterred by Will's silence. "I was only just getting to know Hap, but I already felt that we were making a connection. Don't suppose he mentioned anything about that?"

"What do you want?"

"You know damn well what I want, Detective. And I think you know that Eckhart was gonna give it to me."

Will's knuckles were going white on the receiver. "You got something to say, come out with it."

"Just that I'm looking forward to reading—*carefully* reading—the report on whatever fucking mess went down yesterday."

Will turned from the desk, putting his back to Rachel. He was furious. "Don't *presume* to judge what happened, Warfield. You weren't here. But then you're never here, are you? You're sitting safe behind your fucking desk reading your bullshit reports. And that's why I got nothing but contempt for you and assholes like you who risk *nothing* and spend all day sucking the marrow out of real cops when you never had the balls to be one yourself."

Will slammed down the phone and handed it back to Rachel, who was studying him with a combination of curiosity and bemusement.

"Next time," he told her, "go ahead and lie."

Tonight he was going to sleep. Last night, the vase hadn't worked—despite his efforts, light had still come spilling into his room. But tonight Will had a better strategy. He was a man with a plan. He walked over to his window with the roll of tape he had borrowed from Rachel and pulled down the blind all the way, blocking out the Alaskan night and the creeping silvery light that could drive a person nuts.

Patiently, he taped the blind shut, carefully working around the three loose sides, attaching the blind to the wall and the sill. When he was done, he stepped back. It should have been perfect. But studying the window closely, he found there was still light, an intrusive glow seeping in around the edges!

Where the fuck is it coming from?

Will stepped back another few feet, trying to understand the big picture, the goddamn mystery of why abominably endless daylight could not be shut out from his motel room. He was stepping back when his foot came to rest on the loose floorboard, causing a sudden squeak. This reminded him of other urgent business left for him to do.

Will left the motel on foot, walking down the main street into town. The street was deserted at this hour, after eleven o'clock. It was late for a small country town; most people had probably gone to bed an hour ago. Meanwhile, the sky was unaware of this fact. The heavens glowed like a lit dome overhead, neither day nor night but something hellishly in between.

He kept walking through the deserted streets, passing traffic lights that changed for empty intersections. He passed by a bar, a dive with no win-

dows and a smell of booze and tobacco drifting
out into the street. Inside, there was a sound of
rough laughter and music playing on a jukebox.
Getting drunk was probably the only thing to do
in Nightmute this time of night, for those restless
souls who weren't snug in their beds at home. Will
was sympathetic.

He made his way to the alley where he had
vomited last night. Not exactly a place of fond nos-
talgia, but Will had his reasons. The dead dog was
still sprawled out by the Dumpster, looking even
more awful than before, rancid and rotting. Will
slipped on a pair of latex gloves from his left
pocket. From his right pocket, he pulled out the .38
Smith & Wesson. He looked up the alley; there was
no one around. He took off his coat, wrapped it
around the gun, and fired a single shot into the
dead dog's side. The flesh jumped with the impact,
but the dog was beyond minding.

Will paused, listening for trouble. The shot had
been muffled, but this was not a task at which he
wanted to be caught. He heard nothing except the
bass of the jukebox at the bar up the road. He
found his Swiss Army knife, crouched over the
dog, and set to work. It wasn't a pleasant job, but
he had done worse in his many years of being a
cop. With his gloved fingers, he probed the gash
his shot had made in the dog's side, reaching into
the squishy horror of rotting entrails. It took him
nearly ten minutes, but he found the bullet and

cleaned it up, using rubbing alcohol from a bottle he had bought earlier in the evening.

When he was done, Will had himself a clean .38 slug that could have come from anywhere at all.

In the morning, Will paid a visit to the morgue in the basement of St. Francis Hospital. The harsh fluorescent lights in the hallways assaulted his exhausted eyes. He came through a door and found the coroner pulling a sheet over the cold blue body of Hap Eckhart. Will stopped in his tracks, momentarily unable to move or speak. He felt the coroner staring at him.

"Detective. You came yourself," she said.

Will nodded. He couldn't remember her name. She was just a tall, matronly woman with gray hair who looked more like a librarian than a coroner.

"It's different when you know them, isn't it? Just sign over there," she told him, nodding at a clipboard on the wall. She slipped off her lab coat to reveal a prim blue dress underneath, and headed off into an adjoining office, leaving Will alone with Hap.

Reluctantly, Will approached the body beneath the sheet. It still seemed incredible to him that Hap was dead. Whatever his faults, Hap had always been brimming over with life. Hap the joker. Hap the flirt who could never resist a pretty face. Hap the family man. The sharp dresser. And the son of a bitch who was going to snitch to Internal Affairs just to save his own ass. All these things and more, the contradictions of a human life, gone forever. The sheet over the corpse formed a kind of shroud. Will reached out with his hand and touched the side of his dead partner's head under the sheet.

"I'm sorry!" he whispered.

"He didn't suffer too much." The voice startled him. It was the coroner, coming back into the examining room. She had a small envelope in her hand. It was what Will had come for.

"What caliber?" he asked.

The coroner shrugged. "Wouldn't know. The gunshot victims I see here are from hunting rifles and shotguns. Wasn't one of those."

Will picked up the clipboard, signed his name, and handed it to her, eager to be gone. The coroner took the clipboard and paused to look with concern into his tired, blinking eyes.

"Had any sleep, Detective?"

"Oh, yeah," he answered, trying to make light of it. He reached to take the envelope from her hand. It seemed to him she hesitated slightly before releasing it into his grip, but maybe it was only his overstrained nerves imagining it.

He got out of the morgue, glad to leave the sickening scent of death, as well as his guilt, behind. He started the Cherokee and pulled out of the hospital parking lot. The day was bright and remorseless, not a shred of pollution to gray-down the sky. Pausing for a stoplight, Will opened the envelope in his lap with his free hand and shook out the bullet that had been taken from Hap's gut. It was a 9mm slug from his own gun. The light changed. He pocketed the fatal bullet and drove off, reaching into a different pocket for the bullet he had retrieved from the dog. Fascinating work, rearranging the history of a crime, Will mused. He held the .38 slug up to the light, studying its deadly beauty. Light glinted on the metal, showing clearly the unique pattern of scars, striations marks from the barrel of the gun that had fired it.

Something made him look up. *Fuck!* A woman was crossing the street. Will slammed on the brakes, screeching to a halt. The woman banged her fist on the hood, furious.

"What the hell's wrong with you?" she shouted.

Will shrugged an apology and slipped the .38 slug into the envelope. He had lost his concentration there for a second. But the worst was over. He had taken care of business. Now all he had to do was find Kay Connell's killer, and get the hell back to L.A.

SIXTEEN

Fred Duggar refused to look up when Will came into the bull pen. He had to play his little game, pretending to be engrossed with a sheaf of papers on his desk.

Will tossed the envelope with the .38 slug inside onto Fred's desk.

"I want results by tomorrow morning."

Fred fingered the envelope. "Aye, aye, Cap'n," he answered, managing just the slightest whiff of insolence. "I'm thinking we should check on Randy Stetz's whereabouts yesterday evening."

"You think it was Randy out there?"

"Well, he still doesn't have an alibi for the night Kay was killed," Fred said defensively. "And you're the one saying he beat her up."

The man was a tiring fool. Will nearly said

something cutting, but he let it go. What did it matter if Fred Duggar believed he was God's gift to law enforcement? "Fine," he said. "Check on it."

Will was momentarily unsteady on his feet. All around him, the room was crowded and noisy with bustling activity. Ringing telephones. Loud voices. The *clickety-click* of quick fingers on computer keyboards. The sounds roared in Will's ears, an overload of input. He was feeling fragile as glass.

"Detective Dormer?"

A girl appeared in front of him. For a moment, Will thought it was Hap's daughter, Jenny, somehow grown-up. Then he focused and saw it was Ellie Burr. But she was too young, too bright, too full of energy for his tired eyes.

She smiled and handed him a file. "My report. Just need you to sign it. Take a look, if you've got time."

Will stared without comprehension at the typewritten top sheet. Ellie had put an X where he needed to sign. The text swam in front of his eyes.

"It's pretty straightforward," she told him.

Nothing seemed straightforward to Will at the moment. Still, he took the pen she offered, just to put an end to this.

"I know we've got more important things to worry about than paperwork," she said obligingly. There was a conspiratorial wink in her tone, as if real detectives didn't take paperwork seriously.

Ellie was trying in her way to be one of the guys, a hotshot. She was trying to please him.

Will stopped, pen touching the paper. Ellie's innocence was like a rebuff, bringing him back to his senses. He realized he couldn't lead her astray.

"A man has *died*, Ellie." He handed her back the report, unsigned. "This *is* important."

She looked up into his face, surprised.

"Be sure of all your facts before you file this. It's your name on the report," he told her.

The girl nodded, chastened, which was good. He only hoped in this instance that she wasn't *too* good.

Ellie Burr felt the sting of Will Dormer's reprimand. A flush of embarrassment stayed with her throughout the day, and followed her home that night. She had stupidly tried to adopt a cynical tone just to please Detective Dormer, thinking it would make her fit in. Ellie vowed she would never, *ever* do anything so silly again.

Dormer was right. Her name was on the report. A cop had died and it was her job to make sure she had every fact absolutely accurately right, and that not a single avenue had gone uninvestigated. Nothing was open and shut. She had to think this through from start to finish, look at the shooting from every angle.

After dinner, Ellie watched a TV show with her dad to keep him company. Then she took a

shower, brushed her teeth, and retreated into her
bedroom. She spread out on her floor with the
map of the beach and a stack of photographs that
had been taken of the crime scene. She wondered
if she had missed anything, as she pored over the
evidence.

"You're up late." It was her father, stopping by
her open door, dressed in his pajamas and
bathrobe.

"Looking over some stuff for tomorrow," she
told him. "You take your pills?"

Her dad pulled out a prescription bottle from
his bathrobe pocket, and shook it meaningfully
just to show what a good patient he was. "Don't
stay up too late," he said, heading off down the
hall.

Sprawled out on the floor, Ellie returned her attention to the map and photographs, trying to pretend that she was seeing them for the first time.
Detective Dormer had told her it was the small
things that counted, so she was looking for any
minute detail she might have missed. She went
over everything again from scratch, the chronol-
ogy of events, starting from the moment Farrell
had accidentally triggered the megaphone, alert-
ing the suspect to danger. She took a fresh piece of
paper and made a diagram of where everyone had
gone, and what they had done. The chaos of people moving about in the fog until a shot was fired,

and Farrell was wounded in his thigh. And then another shot, and Hap Eckhart was dead . . .

Ellie yawned, leaning against her bed. She thought as hard as her mind could think. The fishing cabin. The rock where Farrell was wounded. The rock where Will Dormer found his partner dead . . . but it all began to get mixed up in her head, a collage of misty death. She couldn't concentrate. It had been a long day and she was tired. Something stirred in her consciousness, but did not surface.

Ellie drifted, and soon she was fast asleep.

A few miles away, Will Dormer was unable to sleep. He lay in his bed at the Pioneer Lodge wide-awake, more awake than he had been the entire day. It was crazy. The scene was set for sleeping. He had a mattress that wasn't too hard, nor too soft. A fluffy pillow. All the right props.

But still, he just couldn't sleep.

Will groaned in frustration. He turned from his left side to his right, enjoying the coolness of his pillow. Certainly, this should do the trick . . . the crisp smooth sensation of clean linen against his cheek. Only it didn't matter. His eyes remained open. He stared glumly at the window blind that had *looked* dark enough when he had first turned off the lights, but now that his eyes were adjusted, he could make out . . . *for chrissake!* . . . a white glow!

He was getting angry. Fucking insomnia! Will sat up and used the remote to flick on the TV. He watched for a while. It had been a long time since he'd had the leisure to lie in bed and watch TV. Only there was nothing on this time of night, just an infomercial about time-sharing condos in Mexico, and a language class on public television, Italian II. Will Dormer had no need for Italian II, or a time-share in Mexico, so he turned off the television.

He told himself he was ready to sleep. Trying to force himself to be nice and relaxed, he closed his eyes, he snuggled into his pillow. Only there was too much noise. The faint hiss of the radiator. The distant rumbling of the hotel's plumbing. Suddenly—out of nowhere—there was a crackling sound above him, like something terrible being torn in two. Will's eyes popped open in alarm. Horrified, he stared at the ceiling. There was a thin line running in the plaster overhead, a narrow crack. But he could *hear* it—he could hear the crack ripping apart!

Will shut his eyes and turned violently onto his stomach. Night had become his enemy, an implacable foe.

Ellie Burr was asleep on her bedroom floor, stretched out on the carpet. She had always been a girl who could fall asleep instantly anywhere—floor or sofa or chair, it didn't matter. Normally, she would have slept like a baby for a full eight hours and woken refreshed to the bright morning sunshine, unfazed by a night spent on her floor. But tonight was different. Her eyes flickered open.

What was it?

A fleeting thought had awoken her, one that was already half gone. She had to sit up and blink and retrieve the thought from the unconscious darkness in which it was quickly slipping away.

A thought. She had it. She picked up the photographs of the crime scene scattered upon the floor and went through them until she came to one of "Hap" in the water where he had died—it was actually of the officer she had positioned to play Hap, but that didn't matter. Not if she had all her measurements right.

She stared at the photograph, thinking of the bullet and the angle of fire. At last she nodded to herself and said aloud what should have been obvious to her before: *"It couldn't have come from there!"*

Just as Ellie Burr was waking, Will Dormer was finally falling asleep. It was a miracle. All the sounds began fading around him. He felt his muscles relax. Everything was about to slip away when . . . *rrrrrriiinnnnggg!* The telephone on his bedside table exploded to life. Will's eyes snapped open. He was disoriented and it took him a moment to figure out where the noise was coming from.

The phone kept ringing, hellishly. Groggy, he reached over and picked up the receiver.

"Dormer," he managed. His voice was little more than a hoarse croak.

There was a crackle of static on the open line, but no answering voice. Will sat up in bed, fully awake.

"Hello?" he tried.

"Can't sleep?" The speaker was a man. His tone was friendly, almost solicitous, but Will didn't have a clue who he was. "Me neither," the man went on.

"Who is this?"

The man chuckled softly. "I got a nap this afternoon, but I guess you had to work."

"I asked—"

"Get rid of the clock yet?"

Will had figured out by now exactly who it was he had on the line. He opened the drawer of his bedside table and pulled out the digital clock that he had stuffed there. It was 4:17 A.M.

"Doesn't really help," the man was saying. "When I first moved up here I once went five nights. Five nights! Can you believe that? This crazy light . . . but I'm not sure it's the *light* that's keeping you awake."

"A name," Will told him. "Or I'm hanging up."

"No, you're not. You need the company. Nothing as lonely as not sleeping. Feels like the whole planet's deserted. Just you"—the man paused a beat—"and me."

A pleasant voice, without any specific accent. This was no redneck, Will decided. The man was educated and well spoken. "So tell me who I'm talking to and we'll chat awhile."

Again the soft chuckle. "I can't. Not till you understand a couple things."

"Like what?"

"I *saw*, Will."

Will felt suddenly sick to his stomach. "Saw what?" he demanded.

"Saw you kill your partner. Saw you shoot him dead. On that beach. I thought you might try to blame me. That's why I dropped my gun. My uncle's old thirty-eight. Did you pick it up? What about the ballistics? What're you—"

Will interrupted angrily, "Listen, I don't know what you think you saw, but we should discuss this face-to-face—"

"The situation isn't yours to control, Will. I *saw* you do it—get it?"

Will took a breath. He tried to sound confident. "I'll control this situation, pal. You don't hide from me in a town this small."

"No, not for long," the man agreed. "That's why I need your help. So don't worry. I'm not telling anyone anything. We're partners in this."

The line went dead with a click. Will put the

phone down and got out of bed. He began pacing
the floor, his mind racing. He felt like an animal in
a trap. Totally fucked. Suddenly he froze. He had
just heard a sound coming from the next room. . . .
Hap's room! Footsteps shuffled about. For a wild
moment he thought maybe it was a ghost, that
Hap had come back to haunt him. But the footsteps were too solid for any spirit.

Cautiously, Will opened his door to the hallway
and peered down the corridor to Hap's door. He
was thinking of getting his gun when Hap's door
opened and a woman walked out into the hall. It
was Rachel. Will felt his body relax. It was hard to
imagine anyone looking good at four in the morning, but Rachel looked very good indeed. She was
dressed in jeans and a flannel shirt and her long
auburn hair tumbled down her shoulders. She was
lugging two bags, Hap's luggage.

Will made a sound and she jumped. She smiled
when she saw him.

"I tried to be quiet," she told him.

"What are you—"

"They asked me to pack up Detective Eckhart's
things. The day staff said someone's collecting it
tomorrow."

Will nodded. He was in his pajamas and he
thought he should probably go back inside his
room. But he stood there, not moving, wanting her
company.

Rachel's eyes were deep brown and full of sympathy. "Could you give me a hand with these?" she asked.

She could have managed alone; the bags were not very heavy. Will could have gone back into his room to try again to sleep. But instead, he took one of the bags and followed Rachel Clement down to the bar.

SEVENTEEN

The Pioneer Lodge Bar was empty, lost in deep shadows, a single utility light burning against a far wall. To Will it seemed that he and Rachel were the only two people awake anywhere on earth, which made for an odd intimacy. He sat at a table while she poured them both drinks, bourbon and water. Rachel was a woman with perfect instincts. He wished he had met her before things had gone so wrong.

"You knew him a long time?" she asked.

"Partners almost five years."

She came over with their drinks and sat down at the table. They clinked glasses, locking eyes in the semidarkness.

"You must get to know someone real well doing your job."

Will nodded, sipping his drink. "Enough to know his family. His kids."

"His wife must be ..." Rachel struggled for words. "I mean, how do you keep on with everything, for your kids, when you're—"

"Everybody's different," he told her. "In my job, you're always dealing with people who've just lost someone. They're all different. A lot of them don't know how to feel. And it *kills* them. Everybody around them acting like it's obvious what they're going through, but they don't know themselves what they're feeling. Sure they're sad, but it's mixed up with other things."

"How they left things with the person who died?"

Will considered this, taking another swallow of bourbon. "Doesn't always make that much sense," he told her. "I mean, I had a brother who died—"

"I'm sorry—"

"No, it was a long time ago. He died in a fire. And you know what? I was *embarrassed*."

Her brown eyes studied him more closely. "Why?"

He shrugged. "'Cause it made me different. I didn't tell kids at school what happened. They'd ask me where he was and I'd make up stories. He was visiting relatives; he'd broken his leg. Anything but the truth."

Truth! Will thought, realizing the irony. He felt Rachel studying him with more interest than any woman had studied him in a long time. It was nice, but too late. He downed the rest of his drink and stood from the table. "Thanks," he said. He took out some bills from his wallet, but Rachel pushed the money away.

"How long will you stay?" she asked him. It was a simple question, but the way she was looking at him made it more complicated.

"Till I find him," Will answered. "Not long."

One good thing about insomnia was that you didn't need an alarm clock. Will Dormer was looking to accentuate the positive. After leaving Rachel in the bar, he showered, put on clean clothes—a crisp white shirt, a tie, a pair of gray slacks, a dark gray sports jacket—and he was sitting on his bed ready to rumble when the alarm went off at seven-thirty. It was nice to get a head start on the day. Insomnia gave you more time to get everything done.

He stood and examined himself in the mirror. Considering his lack of sleep, he felt better than he had in days. His eyes traveled down his body until he came to the gold badge on his belt. He remembered a time of innocence when that badge had meant everything to him. But being a detective on the L.A.P.D. was not compatible with innocence. After a few years, you began to work the system. The ends justified the means, you told yourself.

But once you wavered, you could never turn around and retrace your steps and be clean again.

Will let out his breath, staring in the mirror at what he had become. Finally, he took the gold badge off his belt, left it on top of the bureau, and went out into the Alaskan morning, determined to find the sick bastard who had telephoned him last night, in the mistaken belief that a compromised cop was easy prey.

The Los Angeles detectives arrive in Nightmute, Alaska.

Detective Will Dormer takes control of the Kay Connell homicide case.

Dormer interrogates Randy Stetz about his whereabouts on the night Kay Connell was murdered.

Blanketed by fog, Will Dormer sets a trap to lure the killer out to a lonely fishing cabin.

Ellie joins the hunt for Finch in the deep Alaskan fog.

Dormer recovers from falling into the icy waters after nearly apprehending the suspect.

Author Walter Finch awaits his rendezvous with Detective Dormer on the ferry.

Dormer and Finch work out a tentative deal.

Dormer questions Finch when he is brought into the police station for questioning.

In order to help prove his innocence, Finch offers to turn over to Ellie letters that Kay Connell had written to him.

Ellie Burr discovers a crucial clue—a bullet slug—at the scene of Detective Hap Eckhart's murder.

Meeting at the Mariners' Monument, Dormer threatens Finch.

Walter Finch's remote house on Lake Kgun.

Finch and his two golden retrievers greet Ellie Burr at the lake house.

Ellie manages to escape out of a window at Finch's cabin.

Christopher Nolan directs Al Pacino during the filming of *Insomnia*.

EIGHTEEN

Kay Connell's funeral took place midmorning in a pretty little cemetery on the edge of town. Located on a small, narrow spit of land that jutted out into the sparkling water, the cemetery was surrounded on either side by the giant, looming mountains, outlined in the background so sharply in the clear air that you could almost make out individual trees. From this side of town, you couldn't see the pulp mill, which added to the tranquility. Will wondered what it would be like to be buried in such a peaceful country spot alongside your grandparents. For himself, he imagined more an incinerator in Los Angeles, flames licking at his bones, the smoke of his body joining the general smog and pollution.

He stood back from the crowd on a small knoll

near the grave of a woman whose name was illegible, 1887–1934. Below him, the crowd consisted of several dozen kids from the high school, some in their Sunday clothes, others at least in their cleanest jeans. There was an equal number of adults, a large turnout. Many of the teenagers were crying—the girls at least, dabbing their eyes with handkerchiefs. Some of them were probably guiltily enjoying the drama. Will was more interested in the adult men. He recognized several teachers he had seen at the high school. Any one of them might have taken a very special interest in a teenage girl. An interest that had somehow turned murderous. Will also noted that Randy and Tanya were standing beside one another, as if they came to the funeral together.

A girl was speaking, standing by the open grave.

". . . but to be remembered as the Kay we knew and loved, swimming, hiking through the Kebaughs, meeting at Darrow's after school. And always, always with a smile on her face."

The girl looked up from her prepared sheet of paper with tears in her eyes. Standing next to her, Mrs. Connell reached over and squeezed her arm. Will wondered if it was true that Kay always, *always* had a smile on her face. He didn't think so, at least not when her boyfriend, Randy, was beating her up. It was the sort of lie people respectfully said at funerals. Meanwhile, a group of young children began handing out white carnations. Will watched as the mourners lined up to place the lush flowers on the casket. Detective Ellie Burr was one of the mourners, dressed in black. Will saw her put down her carnation, then turn and start walking his way.

The ceremony was over and the mourners began drifting away from the grave, some gathering in small groups to talk, others moving slowly toward their cars. Will let his eyes scan the crowd, searching for anything unusual. There was a good chance the killer was present.

Ellie came up to him. "Detective Dormer? I wanted to check something with you."

He glanced at her briefly. She had been crying, which was understandable; she was a cop, but she had also grown up in this town. At the moment, however, Will was more interested in watching the faces of the different people who had known Kay, how they were reacting.

"I was going over my report last night and I have a question about where you think that second shot came from."

Will barely heard her. He had just spotted Kay's best friend, Tanya Francke, the girl with white-blond hair whose photograph had ended up in Kay's wastebasket. Tanya was moving from the grave toward a group of boys. She moved more like a woman than a girl, fully aware of her sexual power.

Ellie was still trying to get his attention, which was irritating. "See," she was saying, "you said you were at the waterline when you heard it, but from the way Detective Eckhart's body fell, I don't think the shot could've come from the rocks farther up from the water."

Will gave Ellie a quick glance, then turned back to Tanya. He knew he needed to respond to Ellie, but he was a lot more interested in Kay's best friend. Tanya had just stopped alongside Randy Stetz.

"Is it possible that you heard the shot *before* you hit the waterline?"

Will watched as Randy jostled Tanya, pretending to bump into her. She turned and an unmistakable look passed between them. It was a look as old as time.

"Detective Dormer?"

Ellie was waiting patiently for his attention. He turned to her reluctantly and tried to remember the last question she had asked. "It's possible," he agreed, and began walking toward where Tanya and Randy were doing their little dance of the birds and the bees.

"Well, are you changing your statement?" she demanded. There was a sharpness in her tone he had never heard before.

He turned back to her. "Yes," he said. She frowned, clearly upset with his behavior. But Will had no time at the moment for Ellie Burr.

He cut across the green lawn past gravestones and small memorials, heading toward the parking lot. A number of mourners were moving in the same direction. A crowd had gathered around Mrs. Connell, awkwardly offering their condolences. Some of the teenage girls were still shedding tears and hugging each other. This was not a day they would ever forget. Will moved past them, closing in relentlessly on Randy and Tanya, who were not crying.

Randy was standing with his back to Will alongside his motorcycle, a big Japanese bike. Randy was spiffed-out in tight jeans and a T-shirt that showed off his muscles. Will imagined Kay was already a distant memory for him. As for Tanya, she stood facing Will, peering over Randy's shoulder. She saw Will and locked eyes with him as he approached.

"Why don't I give her a ride?" Will suggested, joining their little group.

Randy turned and sneered. "Thought I smelled something."

Will smiled. "How are you doing, Randy? Still coping?"

Randy made an elaborate show of ignoring Will. He threw his leg over his bike, strutting his stuff. The show was wasted on Tanya, who had turned her entire attention to Will. Up close, she was a girl of seventeen going on thirty-four. Still attractive, but in a year or two, she would most likely be used up and bitter.

"You're that cop," she said. Not the most intelligent comment in the world, but she imbued it with a certain meaning.

Will returned her look, unsmiling, while Randy stood on the kick starter and jerked down with the weight of his body. As a move, it looked pretty good. Very masculine. But the bike sputtered and died, refusing to respond. "You coming or not?" he said to Tanya. His irritation was beginning to show.

Tanya flicked her eyes from Will to Randy, and back to Will again. Her lips were full of promise, her sullen eyes momentarily aflare with desire for new adventures. Will suspected that fidelity was not one of Tanya Francke's strong points.

As they drove away in the police department Cherokee, Will couldn't help but notice that Tanya's black skirt had slid high up on her thigh in order to give him a maximum view. She had nice legs, long legs that were so youthful it was scary, untouched by sorrow and time. Nevertheless, Will kept his attention on the road.

"Never met anyone from L.A. before," she told him.

"Not missing much."

He felt her eyes upon him, studying him as if he were a puzzle that needed to be solved.

"How do you like our shit-hole town?"

Will shifted gears and glanced over at her. "Were you good friends with Kay?"

"Best friends. Since grade school."

"Long time," he told her. But she missed the sarcasm. Tanya wasn't very bright, only a bored, small-town girl.

"We were like sisters," she added.

"Must be tough for you. What happened."

She put on a serious face. "Everybody keeps telling me I'm doing great, considering. But they're real worried about me. Don't even care if I show up to school or not. They're worried I haven't cried yet."

She stretched. A big theatrical stretch, leaning back in the passenger seat, showing her bare midriff. When she was finished, she turned toward Will.

"But there's no law says you have to cry, right?" she asked.

"What about her other friends?"

Sadly, this line of questioning was starting to bore her. "Do we have to talk about Kay? I don't want to think about all that right now. Let's just drive." She reached over and picked some lint off his shoulder.

Will turned to face her. "You want me to take you someplace?"

Her expression softened. Her hand lingered on Will's shoulder. "Sure. Long as it's fun. Young, im-

pressionable girl left alone with older Los Angeles
cop. Who knows where we might go?"

Will smiled. He shifted gears, accelerating hard.
"I know a place," he said.

Tanya liked excitement and speed, so Will went
fast to please her. He went very fast. They were on
a two-lane road, a ribbon of asphalt that wound its
way up the coast, darting around sudden curves,
coming up over abrupt hills that had spectacular
views of the ocean to the left side of the car. It was
probably a very pretty road, if one was in the
mood to notice the beauty all around.

The speed limit, according to the posted signs,
was thirty-five miles per hour on the straight-
aways, sometimes as low as fifteen on the curves.
Will cruised at sixty. He didn't want Tanya to be
bored. The road straightened and he accelerated to
seventy-five. Tanya giggled happily as the land-
scape rushed past. It probably seemed like the
epitome of freedom to her to fly down the highway with a cop at the wheel—you couldn't even
get a ticket.

But why stop at seventy-five? Or even eighty?
Up ahead, a truck was coming at them from the
other lane. Will was doing close to ninety, drifting
across the double yellow line. The truck beeped its
horn and flashed its headlights to get his attention.
Tanya's giggle died in her throat and she took her
hand from his shoulder.

"Hey!" she cried.

Will ignored her. He felt calm and disconnected. Now *he* was having fun. The truck beeped again, closer.

"Hey, get over!" Tanya shouted. She reached for the wheel, but Will pushed her hands away. The truck was coming up fast.

"Move over, you crazy fuck!" she screamed.

Will waited until the last second, staring death in the face. Then he jerked over into the right lane. The truck roared past, its horn fading. Will downshifted, screeching off the road onto a gravel pulloff in front of a derelict foul swatch of land that was being used as a garbage dump. The Jeep fishtailed to a stop in a cloud of dust, sending garbage flying. Will jumped out and came around to the passenger side, yanking open Tanya's door.

"You fucking asshole!" she cried. "You almost killed us!"

He grabbed her arm and pulled her roughly from the car.

"You're hurting me!"

Will forced her along, pulling her away from the Jeep toward the dump.

"Get off me!" Tanya was nearly hysterical. But Will didn't let up. With a maniacal burst of energy, he hauled her up a trash heap, a mountain of cans and refuse. He didn't stop until they reached the top. Only then did he let go of her arm. The girl's face was set in stone. Apparently this was more adventure than she had bargained for.

"What the fuck is this?" she demanded.

Will was breathing hard. "You and Kay were like sisters?"

"Yes! I told you already!"

"So why's there a torn-up picture of you in her bedroom?"

Tanya stumbled in the garbage. She recovered and shot Will a look of sullen malice.

"Why's her boyfriend's hand clamped on your ass at the funeral?" he demanded. "Randy doesn't have an alibi for Friday. He was with you, wasn't he? You're fucking her boyfriend—that what best friends do?"

Tanya sighed. Like this was really too, too much for her, getting quizzed in such matters of the heart by what she now saw was only a broken middle-aged man, no Romeo who was going to whisk her off to more exciting climes. Will waited for her answer.

"She didn't really love Randy," Tanya managed at last, airily.

"No? How you figure that? She have someone else? Someone who gave her dresses? Jewelry?"

Tanya's expression became sly. But she said nothing. Will was not in the mood for obstruction. He leaned close and lowered his voice dangerously.

"Best friends, huh? You're standing right where

your best friend's naked body was found wrapped in garbage bags."

She looked around at the rotten mound of garbage. She seemed to see it for the first time. A dozen feet away, a seagull was pecking at a dead fish. Tanya turned and tried to run away, down the mound to safety. But Will held on to her. When she looked at him again, her eyes were full of terror. He had her attention, at least.

He spoke more softly. "Tanya, I know you don't want anybody knowing that you betrayed your friend. I know that's why you can't give Randy his alibi. Tell me who Kay was seeing and you won't have to. It'll be our secret. But I need a name."

Tanya stared at the seagull and the dead fish. She was close to tears. "She wouldn't tell me, okay?"

"You were best friends," Will pressed.

"It was her big fucking secret!"

"Why?"

"She thought she was special. She kept saying she was gonna get out of here. That *he* was gonna help her."

"*Who?*"

"She never said!"

"But you *talked* about him."

"She didn't use his name!"

"But what did she call him?"

"Brody. She called him Brody. But that isn't his fucking name so what's the difference?"

Brody? Will let Tanya break free of his grip while he stood thinking. He was certain he had come across that name recently, but for the moment he couldn't remember where. At another time in his life, younger and with much more sleep, his brain had been a more reliable instrument.

Tanya stumbled down off the mound of garbage, anxious to be as far away from him as possible.

"Happy now, you fucking asshole?" she screamed.

Happy was not the word Will would have used to describe himself. Mystified, perhaps. But at least the morning hadn't been a complete waste.

Brody. The name meandered around the tunnels of his memory, seeking to make a connection.

NINETEEN

Will found the bull pen deserted, except for Rich, one of the officers, who was busy working on something on his computer terminal. The phones were quiet and a sleepy afternoon stillness had settled over the station. Will was glad for a moment of peace. He needed to think. And remember.

Brody! Where had he heard that name before?

He pulled a cardboard evidence box down from a shelf. In L.A., they had separate storage areas for evidence and heavy locks on the door, but things were much more casual here. Will put the box on one of the desks and cut open the seal. Inside he found the contents of Kay Connell's knapsack. He brought out her belongings one by one—a paperback novel, several textbooks—until

he came to her diary. He began flipping through
the pages, reading at high speed, looking for a
single name.

"Just poetry," said a voice, coming up behind
him. It was Ellie. She was starting to feel like his
shadow, showing up unexpectedly. "I went
through it line by line. There's nothing specific.
Verses about nature, love, that stuff."

Will nodded. He had been reading through her
adolescent rhymes—nothing profound, but simply the fact that she would write poetry gave him
a new take on Kay. Randy certainly would not be
spending his free time in such a way, and neither
would Tanya Francke. In a small town like Nightmute, Alaska, Kay would have been an anomaly.
Decidedly out of place. She probably couldn't
wait to get the hell away from here to someplace
more cultured. And according to Tanya, this person Brody was going to help her get away. . . .

Will was deep in thought when the phone
rang. Rich picked up his extension and spoke to
someone on the other end. "Detective Dormer?"
he called. "Line one."

Will shook himself out of his reverie and
picked up the phone. "Dormer," he said crisply.

"Three nights without sleep. Can't be easy to
keep working."

Will was instantly on guard. It was the voice
from last night. He did not reply.

"I mean, are you seeing things yet?"

Will glanced about the office nervously. Ellie had returned to her desk, but she was looking at him. He felt trapped, closed in on all sides. Meanwhile, the man on the other end kept talking, his voice relaxed and easy. As if they were connected in some way. Old friends.

"Tricks of the light, little flashes? You seeing Eckhart? . . . I see Kay sometimes."

"What can I do for you, sir?" Will managed.

"I got a question for you."

"Uh-huh."

"Why couldn't you tell anyone you shot your partner?"

Will kept his silence. Idly, he closed the diary and put it back inside the evidence box. Kay's other things were on the table. He picked up the textbooks and put them in the box as well, then reached for the paperback novel.

"I mean, it *was* an accident, right?" the man asked him.

"You should hope so, don't you think?"

Will stared at the cover of the paperback. *Otherwise Engaged:* Another J. Brody Mystery.

Brody! There it was. So Brody was a character in a book?

"No need for threats," the voice was telling him, unruffled. "I'm just trying to make you understand my situation. See, you thought no one would believe you. Because of the trouble in Los Angeles, right?"

Will had found the name of the author. Walter Finch. He flipped the book over and scanned quickly over the copy on the back cover describing the exciting plot. He came to a capsule biography of the author at the bottom. It was only a single sentence, but for Will it was solid gold:

Mr. Finch now lives in Umkumiut, Alaska, with his two golden retrievers, Lucy and Desi.

"I know what that's like, Will," the man was saying. "I've got the same problem. I'm not who you think I am."

"No?" Will wrote the name of the town, Umkumiut, on a scrap of notepaper.

"I'm not a murderer. Any more than you are."

"So let's get together. A few beers . . ."

But he was talking into a dead line. The mystery man had hung up. Will put down his receiver and stood up. It was definitely time to pay a visit to Mr. Walter Finch of Umkumiut, Alaska.

"Got some things to check out," he told Ellie. He pointed to the box. "Let's get that stuff back into evidence."

"Are we done with her diary? Her mother might like it back."

He nodded. "Tell Fred we'll catch up tomorrow morning," he said in motion, walking quickly from the room.

Ellie watched him leave. Her eyes felt like

sharp little question marks digging into the back of his spine.

Will followed a two-lane highway north toward the town of Umkumiut, which according to his map was about fifteen miles up the coast. The ocean darted in and out of view as the highway crossed a thousand little fingers of land, winding its way up the jagged coastline. It was late afternoon and the slant of summer sunlight made everything as beautiful as a poster in a travel office. This was the idyllic scenery people came to Alaska to see. Will imagined it would be swell to be a tourist here, instead of a cop.

He had the .38 Smith & Wesson revolver wrapped up in a piece of cloth on the passenger seat of the Cherokee. If all went well, he'd return the weapon to its owner, and then, forensically speaking, everything would be right as rain—a puzzle with all its pieces in place that even Detective Fred Duggar would be able to solve. Meanwhile, his eyes stung from lack of sleep. He stopped at a convenience store a few miles out of Umkumiut and bought a large black coffee that tasted like hot cardboard. The caffeine didn't wake him so much as jangle his nerves and turn his stomach into a maelstrom of acid.

A half block farther up the main drag, he pulled into a gas station that had a telephone booth outside, a historical relic of simpler times.

In cities like L.A., telephone booths had long since disappeared, due to the propensity of homeless people to take up residence in any kind of structure, however small. Will parked and flipped open the phone book to "F." He forced his tired eyes to focus on the small print, moving down the column until he found the name he was seeking: WALTER FINCH, 451 S. DIAMOND TOOTH, APT. 12.

The highway curved and dove over a wooded hill into a pretty little town that looked like an advertisement for the Last Frontier. Umkumiut had a single main street with cute cafés and gift shops and art galleries. There were towns like this all over America—up and down the California coast, just the same as the Alaskan coast: Towns that lived off tourism and the sale of arty little knick-knacks, and second homes to which people eventually retired, seeking to "get away from it all." Will pulled around the side of a tour bus that was disgorging a human stream of Lower Forty-eighters with camcorders in hand. They all seemed to be wearing funny hats and brand-new white tennis shoes.

Will got onto South Diamond Tooth Road and drove the short distance to number 451, a stark two-story apartment building that had no tourist charm. Judging from the building, Walter Finch had not yet made the *New York Times* bestseller list with his J. Brody mysteries. Will parked across the street and approached warily. He was awake now, his adrenaline firing.

Will entered a small, shabby lobby and made his way down a long, narrow corridor to number 12. There were cooking smells in the hallway and the raucous sounds of TV emanating through the thin walls. But number 12 was quiet. Will paused and listened, unbuttoning his coat so he could get to his gun easily. He knocked on the door. There was no response. He waited, then knocked again. Walter Finch did not appear to be at home.

Will examined the door. There was a small, brightly colored piece of paper wedged near the top of the frame, designed to drop should any uninvited guest disturb the door. Walter, it seemed, was a student of crime novels. However, a piece of paper wasn't going to stop Will. He glanced up and down the hall. He saw no one, so he pulled out a credit card from his wallet and went to work on the lock, slipping the plastic into the crack along the doorframe. It was a cheap lock, not difficult to jimmy open. The piece of paper dropped as he opened the door, a scrap torn from a comic book. Will picked it up and set it on a hall table just inside the apartment.

He stood in the open doorway, getting a fix on Walter Finch's world. The place was cheaply furnished with tables and chairs and lamps that might have come from a thrift store, secondhand. There were thin beige patterned curtains on the windows. A TV that looked like a remnant from the dawn of technology. An easy chair with old stains on the arms facing the television. Will heard the two dogs before he saw them, their collars jangling as they came his way from another room. They were huge golden retrievers and they pranced his way, growling deep in their throats. Fortunately, Will was prepared for them. He pulled out a handful of dog biscuits from his coat pocket.

"Hey, Lucy! Desi!" He put on his friendliest man-loves-dog voice. The dogs came forward suspiciously, but food was clearly the path to affection. The growls ceased and soon they were wagging their tails, looking up at him with eager, innocent faces. Will put down a few biscuits on the carpet and moved out of the way as they trotted over and gobbled up the treats. When the dogs were taken care of, he crossed the room and continued to get the lay of Walter Finch's apartment. It wasn't much. Besides the living room, there was a small bedroom, a narrow kitchenette, a windowless bathroom, and several closets. Everything was crowded, cluttered, and in need of a feminine hand, not to mention a good cleaning. There was a tangible aura of loneliness everywhere he looked. Will wondered how many lonely rooms he had searched through in his police career, the temporary dwellings of too many desperate, displaced people.

He wandered back into the living room. There was a desk in the corner with papers and a typewriter. No sign of a computer, which made Walter part of a dwindling breed. On the wall next to the desk there was corkboard with newspaper clippings tacked up. Will scanned the headings. They were all about cops. OFFICER LOUIS SAVED MY LIFE! SHOOTOUT IN SOHO. SOUTH STREET COP TAKES DOWN DRUG RING. LOS ANGELES DETECTIVE KILLED BY CONNELL SUSPECT.

Will's eyes dropped to the desk itself. On one corner there was a neat stack of eight-by-ten black-and-white photographs—signed author photos. Will lifted the top picture and found it was gritty with a layer of dust. Apparently Finch didn't have a huge number of fans screaming for his portrait. The photograph was pretentious, the author in a three-quarter profile looking like the camera had caught him in a moment of profound inspiration. There was a lake with a glacier rising up from it in the background. From the photograph, Finch appeared to be a middle-aged man—mid-forties, Will guessed. He was neither handsome nor plain, the sort of man it was hard even to describe. Just average, someone who would melt into any crowd, unnoticed. Light brown hair, Will decided, studying the black-and-white photo. A prominent nose and jowly cheekbones. But otherwise a face you could forget instantly. A mousy little man who also just happened to be a murderer.

Will pulled a clean photograph from the stack and replaced the dusty one on top of the pile. He was folding the picture when he heard the dogs move, heading for the door. They were wagging their tails in greeting and making little squealing sounds of joy. Through the crack at the bottom of the door, Will could just make out the shadow of two feet. Will waited but the door did not open. He remembered the small scrap of comic book on the table; he had planned to replace the paper outside the door when he left, but it was too late now. He flung himself into motion, leaping across the room. He tore open the front door, but the dingy corridor was empty. He heard a sound of running footsteps disappearing around the corner. Will ran in pursuit, flying down the hall. But he wasn't fast enough. He turned the corner just in time to see a door to the outside swing shut.

Will burst out of the building. The sidewalk outside was busy with tourists—a crowd of people with blank faces who seemed to be wondering where the next souvenir could be found. Will looked up and down the street, frantically trying to find Walter Finch. A motion caught his eye. He turned and saw a group standing in front of a souvenir shop, several houses down the road, a figure weaving through their midst. *Finch?* Will hurried after him, racing down the sidewalk. The figure up ahead reached an intersection and cut right, around the glass corner of a shop front. Will was close behind. He came up to the corner in time to find that the man had stopped and turned to see if he was being pursued. They made eye contact through two panes of glass. It *was* Walter Finch. As soon as he saw Will, he bolted away.

Will raced around the corner into the side street. But Walter had disappeared, vanished. Will kept going in the direction he must have taken, running as fast as he could. He came to a back alley between houses that looked promising. And yes . . . there he was, jumping a gate at the end of the alley into someone's yard. Will ran after him, kicking over a trash can, launching himself over the gate, landing out of breath. Finch was at the far end of the yard, climbing over a back fence. Will went after him, leaping over the fence, skidding down a steep incline.

They were at the edge of town. Finch was maybe thirty yards ahead, sprinting across a clearing toward a line of trees. Will was exhausted but he refused to give up. He ran for all he was worth, a pain cutting into his side. Finch disappeared into the trees. Will followed, jogging through the trees until he came to a recently cleared forest. There were blackened stumps, sawdust everywhere, a stack of huge logs. For a moment, Will thought he had lost the author, but

suddenly there he was, at the far side of the clearing, running toward a river.

I got you now, shithead! Will slowed down,
catching his breath. He had Finch up against the
river—a serious body of water, with no place to
escape. But then the craziest thing happened.
Walter Finch began walking across the water! Did the
guy have magic powers, or what? Will sprinted
across the clearing to the riverbank and he soon
had a better idea of how this could be. The river
was a sea of logs, huge cut trees that were floating ponderously downstream. Walter was
halfway across to the far bank, stepping from log
to log. He made it look easy.

Will hesitated on the bank. He suspected it
wouldn't be fun to fall off one of these floating
logs into a river of dangerously churning water.
But how hard can it be? If Walter Finch could do it,
he could, too. There wasn't any choice. Will
jumped from the bank onto a monstrous moving
tree. The log immediately began turning on him
underfoot. He flailed his arms, nearly losing his
balance, but managed to spring onto the next
tree. The footing was slick and treacherous, but
he soon got the general idea of log walking. You
needed to keep going, hardly touching down, de-
fying gravity and common sense—if you lingered
too long on any single log, the thing started twisting on you, and you were lost.

A logjam! He had never before pictured the reality of a swollen river full of trees that were in constant motion—tons of wood that was separating, drifting, spinning, and slamming together. The noise on the river was deafening, the sound of the river itself and all the logs crashing together. Will kept going, hopping from one massive tree to another. At first, he kept his attention close at hand, looking either at the log he was on, or to the next log over where he wanted to go. Finally, more confident, he dared to raise his eyes to see where he was. He was about halfway across. That was the good news. The bad news was that Walter Finch had already arrived at the far bank, and had turned to look at him, smiling mischievously. Will stared back angrily. But it was a mistake to take his concentration from the twisting log on which he stood, even for a second. The log turned and before he knew what was happening, Will slipped off his rolling perch into the icy water.

He cried out in pain and surprise, smashing his ribs against something hard. The water was murky and deathly cold. Will felt himself being dragged down by the weight of his shoes and clothes. He opened his eyes underwater and tried not to panic. Above him, he could see logs stretching into the distance. Shafts of light broke through as the gaps between logs opened and closed. He thrashed his way upward, reaching with his hand for the underside of a log, searching for an opening.

And there it was: a gap! He thrust his head above water, gasping for air, looking about wildly. He saw a sudden movement beside him and went underwater just in time as two great logs came together. *Boom!* The sound was concussive. He had to get away from here, back to the bank. He turned in what he hoped was the right direction and began swimming beneath the logs, moving his arms and feet with all his strength. He was a good swimmer from growing up near the beach in L.A., but this time he was swimming for his life.

He could see the bank. A few more yards and he was in shallow mud among tree roots. He pulled himself out of the water, his lungs rasping for breath as he hauled himself onto the shore. For some time he could only lie on his stomach, shivering and trying desperately to get enough air. His ribs hurt from where he had been banged against a log. Slowly, he managed to get to his knees and rise to his feet. He saw that he was back on the side of the river where he had begun. Walter Finch stood on the opposite bank staring at him.

Will pulled out his .45 automatic and pointed it angrily across the river. But it was hopeless. Water flowed from the barrel and the distance was too great for a handgun. Frustrated, Will lowered his pistol and looked down at himself. He was soaking wet and filthy, and his arm was gashed and bleeding. He was a mess.

All he could do was watch as Walter Finch, on the far side of the river of floating logs, waved to him cheerfully, then turned and walked away.

TWENTY

Will's ribs hurt like hell as he limped back from the river to Walter Finch's apartment on Diamond Tooth Road. With every step he experienced a fresh jolt of pain. He was cold and miserable and angry. But the anger kept him going.

He went first to the Jeep to fetch the .38 Smith & Wesson, which was wrapped up in material in the front seat. Luckily, the street in front of the apartment building was completely deserted. God only knew where all the tourists had gone. They were probably back at their Triple-A recommended motels, safe and sound.

Will went back inside Finch's building, alert for danger. The door to apartment 12 had been left ajar from when Will had run out earlier on his merry chase into the log-jammed river. Still, he wasn't taking any chances. He drew his own .45, now dry, and entered cautiously. The two dogs, Lucy and Desi, sat on their haunches and stared at him curiously, no longer alarmed by his presence. Will closed the door behind him silently and made an inspection of the apartment. He didn't relax until he was certain that Finch was not at home. He was in the bathroom, pulling a towel from the rack and kicking off his soggy shoes, when the phone rang. The sound made him jump.

The phone rang three times and then an answering machine clicked on. Will drifted out of the bathroom toward the machine, which was sitting on the desk in the home office in the corner of the living room. He listened to Walter Finch's familiar voice coming through the speaker, but did not pick up.

"Will? Are you there?"

Will sighed, wiping his face with the towel.

"Where else could you go in that state?" Walter was asking, his voice full of concern. "If you want, take a shower. Should be clean towels in the bathroom."

Will dropped the towel from his neck onto the floor, wanting no part of Walter's hospitality. He listened as the machine clicked off. A few seconds later, the phone rang again. It was Walter.

"Will, pick up. Look, I'm not dumb enough to come back there now—"

Will grabbed the receiver. "Walter Finch," he said coldly.

"Will? What were you doing? I'm trying to *help* you, and you're running around like a maniac. Were you gonna kill me? How would you explain that?"

"No one gets too upset when a child-killer's brought in feetfirst."

"There's no evidence that I killed Kay," Finch replied patiently. Nothing seemed to ruffle him. "You only know it 'cause I told you what I saw out on the beach. Come on, what's wrong with you?"

Will grinned, suddenly punchy. "Guess I'm a little cranky," he admitted. "Lack of sleep, you know?"

"Well, get some rest, will you? I've got some pills in the bathroom cabinet. And my bed's nice and comfy. Go get your head down." Finch was starting to sound like his mother. Will was disgusted with himself that he was even listening to the creep. "Another night up and you're really gonna lose it—hallucinating, babbling, God knows. Get some sleep, and tomorrow when you're feeling better we'll meet. In public. Sort things out. There's a ferry about five miles north of Nightmute. I will be on the eleven o'clock. And Will . . . ?"

Will refused to answer.

"Before you leave, could you feed the dogs? They haven't had—"

Will hung up midsentence. He stared at the phone for a second, then used the towel to wipe it clean of his prints.

Will felt slightly more human a half hour later. He had used Finch's shower, hanging up his damp clothes from the curtain rod on the front window, giving them a full blast of late-afternoon sun through the glass.

Meanwhile, he planned to have the last word when it came to dealing with the child-killing crime writer. He took the .38 from where he had left it on the hall table and began looking about for a good hiding spot. He wanted someplace convincing, where Finch might have put the weapon after killing Hap, but not so clever that the Nightmute police wouldn't be able to find it. He settled on a heating vent that was at floor level in the living room, unscrewing the metal grille with his Swiss Army knife. He made sure the .38 was free of his own prints, giving it another careful wipe, then slipped it down into the heating duct. When he finished screwing the grille back into place, he stood up and saw that the two golden retrievers were watching him patiently, sitting on their haunches, hoping for dinner.

He shook his head at them. They expected him to *feed* them? It was crazy! No fucking way!

And yet . . . he still had some slightly soggy dog biscuits in his pocket. What the hell? He dropped them on the ` floor and fled Walter Finch's lonely world.

Will had another sleepless night, but he was used to that. Go without sleep long enough, and the world takes on a strange clarity. He felt horrible, and had ever since Hap died. Every day, his face seemed to draw more gaunt, his steps becoming more plodding and lifeless.

In the morning, he drove to the station, parked, and made his way into the bull pen. He needed to walk carefully so as not to jostle his ribs too much, but the pain added to his misery. He took in everything at a glance, like some omniscient god. Ellie was at her desk in the corner, poking and pecking at her typewriter. Fred was at the next desk over. He looked up.

"Got a fax from the lab," Fred told him. "Murder weapon was a thirty-eight Smith & Wesson."

Will took the fax from Fred and pretended it was news. Walter Finch didn't know it yet, but justice was tightening around him like a noose. Will continued toward the coffee machine across the common room, thinking he might want to add to his tremendous clarity.

"We found something else, might be worth checking out," Fred said. "Ellie was over—"

"I was at Connell's," Ellie interrupted. "And I found this book."

Fred held up what Ellie had found. It was a hardcover edition of *Otherwise Engaged* by Walter Finch. Will stared at the cover, trying to keep his expression neutral.

"And?" he asked.

Ellie gave him a surprised look.

"*And*," she said, "it's by the same author as the paperback in Kay's backpack."

Fred opened the cover. "It's signed by the author."

Will watched Fred flip the book over and hold up the back cover. There was a picture of Walter Finch, the pretentious photo of the author in profile with a lake and a glacier behind him.

"Turns out he's a local writer," Fred said.

"Kay had all his books," Ellie added.

Will sipped his coffee, wondering how he should play this. He had planned to lead them to Walter eventually, but not this soon. Not until after they met today and he was sure he had the author completely neutralized.

"Don't you think we should check it out?" Ellie asked. There was a hint of sarcasm in her tone. "Small stuff, right?"

Will saw there was no way he could keep her away from investigating Finch. "Sure," he said, trying to be agreeable. "You're right. Good work, Ellie." He turned to Fred. "Kid's got sharp eyes, huh?"

Will turned to pour himself more coffee, as though he had nothing more worrisome to think about than whether someone needed to make a fresh pot. But he saw a look in Ellie Burr's eyes that bothered him.

TWENTY-ONE

WIll drove up the coast to the ferry station south of Umkumiut, where Walter Finch—author and killer of Kay Connell—made his home.

The eleven o'clock ferry was waiting at the end of the pier, its engine idling, loading a line of cars. Most of the passengers were tourists who had come to enjoy the splendid natural setting, a deep-water bay with mountains on the far side—distant peaks that floated upward to a glacier that was sparkling white against an impossibly blue sky. Will bought a ticket and just made it on board, the last passenger before the sailors shut the gates and untied the ropes.

It was a big white boat with several levels of decks with benches for passengers to sit, both in-doors and out. The engine vibrated underfoot as the ferry headed out slowly onto the bay. Before long, they were pitching gently, riding the swells, the bow sending up a spray of salt water as it plowed through the waves. Will weaved through the crowd of tourists in search of Finch, starting in the passenger area on the lowest deck, then working his way upward. He passed a snack bar, where they sold sandwiches and soft drinks, and kept walking up the aisles of seats. He spotted Finch standing by a large window near the bow of the boat admiring the view. Will moved beside him. The author was dressed in a flowery sports shirt, jeans, and a tan corduroy jacket, looking like someone on vacation who didn't have a care in the world. He was shorter than Will had imagined from their hellish chase yesterday, not physically impressive. *Nebbishy*.

"When I was seven my grandmother took me to Portland," Walter said pleasantly, without looking around. "We were walking along when these two men ran past, snatched her purse. That night a police officer came to our hotel room to ask us questions. Stood the whole time. His uniform looked brand-new, shoes and badge polished. Billy club and belt buckle. All perfect. Like a soldier, but better."

Walter stopped to pull out a tissue and blow his nose. Will stared at his hands, appalled. The author's knuckles were red and swollen, probably from beating Kay Connell to death. Will felt a dizzy rush of adrenaline. He wanted to slam Finch up against the window and cinch his cuffs around the other man's wrists way too tight. But he couldn't do a thing without conclusive proof.

Finch kept talking, as if Will would be interested in his bullshit. "I have great respect for your profession," he was saying. "That's why I write about it. I actually tried to become a cop after high school, but"—he paused, reliving an old disappointment—"I couldn't pass all the tests."

"Should've tried out for I.A. They would've taken you," Will quipped.

At last, Finch turned to face Will directly. "I'm not who you think I am."

"No? Walter Finch: shitty writer, lonely freak"— Will lowered his voice—"killer."

Walter shook his head, as though saddened that Will should think such a terrible thing about him. The ferry's engines, working at full speed, sent a shudder up into the ship.

Finch had brought him on the only transport to the Gendreau Glacier, a river of blue ice that spilled down between two mountains now visible ahead on the bay. The tourists nearby were taking pictures like crazy, posing their wives and children, hoping to capture the immensity of this natural setting in the narrow viewfinders of their instamatics and camcorders. The glacier would probably be more real to them a few months from now when they were back home looking at their TV sets and photo albums, rather than at that moment, with the giant cascade of ice sweeping down in front of them.

Walter enjoyed playing tour guide. "You know this glacier flows constantly? In summer it can move a couple inches a day. All that pressure! So slow. You can hear it cracking. Listen."

"What do you want from me, Finch?"

Walter hesitated. They had stayed back from the crowd on the ferry, allowing themselves some privacy to talk. "When Kay died, I knew everyone would think I *meant* to do it. So I cleaned the body, removed any evidence that might connect me."

Will laughed unpleasantly. "Except your fucking novel!"

"Under pressure, you can't always see the wood for the trees." His tone was barbed. "You, of all people, should've figured that out by now."

Will's smile faded.

"When I heard that someone had come up from Los Angeles, I panicked," Finch confided happily, now that they were such good friends. "The local cops didn't scare me. . . . I knew they'd connect me to Kay eventually, but I could handle them. They never look into the eyes of a killer. And killing changes you. You know that. Cop like you, you'd see it right away, wouldn't you?" Walter turned his gaze up to the glacier, but he seemed to be looking inward. "It's not guilt. . . . I didn't *mean* to kill her.

It's more like awareness—life's so important. . . . How can it be that fragile . . . ?"

"You're trying to impress the wrong guy, Finch. Killing that girl made you feel special, but you're not. You're the same distorted, pathetic freak I've been dealing with for thirty years. You know how many of you I've caught with your pants down?"

"I never touched her like that!"

"But you wanted to," Will pressed. "And now you wish you had. Best you could do was clip her nails."

Walter shook his head vehemently, hurt and angry by what Will was saying.

"So now you're different. Blah, blah, blah!" Will's voice was heavy with loathing. "Don't you get it? You're my *job*, Finch. You're as mysterious to me as a blocked toilet is to a fucking plumber. I could care less about your *reasons* for what you did."

Walter smiled, sensing a crack. "Motivations are *everything*, Will." He paused meaningfully. "I mean, what *did* you see through that fog? I saw things pretty clearly, didn't I? I saw you take aim—"

"Forget it, Finch."

"I saw you blast him in the gut. What was it? Was he gonna throw you to Internal Affairs? It's all in the newspapers . . . all that *tension* in your department!"

Will smiled. "You think I'm that easy?"

"I just mean that's how it looks." Walter moved closer, full of empathy. "Might even be how it *feels*? You know? How *did* it feel? When you saw it was Hap? Was it guilt . . . relief?"

Will shook his head, trying to pretend this wasn't getting to him.

"Suddenly free and clear!" Walter whispered, putting his hand on Will's arm. "Had you thought about it before? About how it would be if he just wasn't there anymore? That doesn't mean you did it on purpose, you know."

Will smacked Walter's hand away. "You think because you've got something on me I'm gonna roll over to protect my reputation?"

"To protect your *work*," Walter told him, amazed that Will couldn't see what was so obvious. "All those scumbags you put away—back on the streets before you even get to trial. Look, Hap's dead. You're free and clear. Why mess with that?"

Will answered with a single name: "Kay Connell."

Walter was exasperated. "Your choice. But think of all the other Kay Connells. You're a pragmatist. You have to do your job." He moved closer and softened his tone. "I know this isn't easy for you. That's why I'm trying to make you understand we're in the same boat. I didn't *mean* to kill Kay any more than you *meant* to kill Hap. No one would believe either of us. We need each other. We've got to find a patsy for the Connell case and make it stick. Then you can go back to Los Angeles and I can get on with my life."

Will made a show of thinking it over, as if he were fresh out of options—which was very nearly the truth. He took a deep breath.

"What do you need from me?" he asked.

"Do they know about me yet?"

Will nodded. "They found a signed copy of one of your books at Kay's house. You'll be brought in for questioning."

"At the station?"

Will nodded again.

"Okay." Walter was thinking. "Brought in for questioning. Good. I can write this."

"Take it easy," Will advised. "It'll just be a preliminary inquiry. Tell the truth about your relationship with Kay. Don't try to hide it. It's too obvious."

"I'll tell them about Randy. About how he—"

"No," Will said. "Don't talk about anyone else."

"But I should suggest that she was unhappy. Afraid of *someone*?"

Will agreed. "But let them do the rest," he said. "Let them come to Randy themselves. That way they'll make it stick."

Walter considered this. He seemed excited, as if it were just the sort of clever thing he might think up for the plot of one of his crime novels. Meanwhile, the ferry blew its horn, getting ready to dock at the foot of the giant glacier.

"Then we'll need the wild card," Walter said with a cagey smile as they were walking toward the ferry's ramp.

"Wild card?"

"Something we can use. Something already there. Every good detective story has one." He thought a moment. "Do you still have the thirty-eight?"

Innocently, Will shook his head.

"Shame," Walter said. "We need something solid like that. Something that would totally convince them." They had come to the dock, the tourists already streaming toward the gatehouse, where a ranger was taking tickets to tour the glacier. "Take the next one. We shouldn't be seen together before the questioning."

Will shrugged. He supposed it was a good point. He watched as Walter gave his ticket to a man at the gate. The horn sounded again, high and clear in the mountain air. Will was turning to walk away on the ferry deck when he heard Walter call his name.

"Dormer!"

Will turned back to the shore. Walter was by the dock. The boat's engines were churning up water, about to pull away. With a big smile on his face, Walter pulled out a minicassette recorder from his pocket. He held it up for Will to see. *Wild card!*

Will began to bolt toward the ramp, but he stopped, knowing it was impossible to get ashore.

"Too late," he said.

Which was an understatement. Will Dormer's best hope to nail Kay Connell's killer with the planted .38 in the heating vent had just crashed and burned, leaving him with nothing.

TWENTY-TWO

Ellie Burr stayed late at the station that evening. At eight o'clock she was still at her desk, idly bouncing a tennis ball on the floor, going over everything in her mind.

A vague unease wore at her.

Bounce!

She stared at the map on her desk, the beach where Hap Eckhart had died.

Bounce!

She had studied the map so many times that she hardly even saw it anymore. Everything was engraved in her mind. The angle of the bullet that had killed Detective Eckhart, where it must have been fired from.

Bounce!

Ellie had drawn a line on the map. The trajec-

tory of the fatal bullet passed very close to the red
X that marked the spot where Will Dormer had
been standing.

Bounce!

But that didn't make any sense. Will and Hap
were partners, close friends. What motive would
he have to kill his own partner?

Bounce! But this time the tennis ball didn't return. A hand had darted out from behind, grabbing it. Ellie looked up to see Francis standing by
her desk with a teasing smile and her tennis ball in
his hand. She hadn't heard him.

"Working overtime?" he asked, tossing the ball
to Rich, who was across the room by the gun cabinet.

"Cracking some big cases?" Rich taunted. As
teasing went, this was gentle. But still patronizing.
"Go deep!" Rich called to Francis, pretending to
throw the tennis ball like a football. Francis
slalomed around the desks in the bull pen, making
his way to the back of the room.

"Guys!" she pleaded. But they were having too
much fun at her expense to stop. Rich threw the
ball to Francis, who missed the catch—he had
never been much of an athlete. The ball thumped
off corkboard on the wall and dropped down behind a file cabinet. Ellie glared at Rich, disgusted.
Rich only shrugged and moved back to his desk to
get to work, the game over. It really pissed her off
that neither of them took her seriously, even

though she was a detective, outranking them both. It was probably her own fault. She didn't have enough . . . what was the word her World Lit teacher had used at the community college? *Gravitas.* She forgot exactly what it meant, but whatever it was, she knew she didn't have it.

Ellie was tempted to tell Rich and Francis to get her goddamn tennis ball. But that would have caused a confrontation, and she didn't like confrontations. So she ended up doing it herself. She took a ruler from her desk and knelt down by the side of the file cabinet. She could see the ball, wedged in between the cabinet and the wall. There was something else there as well, an old newspaper. She reached with the ruler—it was a stretch, but she managed to poke at the tennis ball until it rolled her way. For good measure, she fished the newspaper out as well. To her surprise, it was a copy of the *Los Angeles Times.* She couldn't imagine how an *L.A. Times* had made its way up to Alaska, only to lose itself behind a file cabinet at the Nightmute police station. The headline read: DEEPER INVESTIGATION INTO ROBBERY HOMICIDE.

She carried the newspaper and tennis ball back to her desk. She remembered now—Hap Eckhart had the Los Angeles paper with him on the morning when she had met the two detectives at the floatplane. It seemed like an eternity ago. She had brought them directly to the station that day, and

Hap had most likely set down his paper on the file cabinet, then forgotten about it.

Ellie unfolded the *Times* and read the lead story, curious about life in far-off Los Angeles. One front-page story concerned a major Internal Affairs investigation into corruption at the L.A.P.D. Her heartbeat quickened.

It was another terrible night at the Pioneer Lodge. A white night, Alaskan style, but Will Dormer was ready for it.

Twack!

He had a hammer and nails and an extra blanket he had ripped off his bed. There were times when a guy needed to be resourceful. He nailed the blanket up over the window in his room, shutting out the light. A drastic step, but Will meant business. His eyes were wet and heavy with exhaustion. He was asleep on his feet. *Twack!* He hammered another nail in, setting the blanket in place. Perfect.

Will was in bad shape. Waking dreams and hallucinations tumbled through his head. He kept fading in and out of time. One moment, he was there in his room—reality?—then it was as if fog had gathered around him and he was back on the beach again, the goddamn beach near the fishing cabin, plunging over the rocks, his gun raised. It started happening just as it had happened before. A figure up ahead, ghostly in the mist. He raised his arm, took aim . . . but he could see the figure more clearly. They locked eyes together: the man who was about to die with the man who was about to shoot him . . . *and it was Hap!* No question at all: Hap was staring at him across the smoky mist.

Could Will change what had happened? Revise the past? It was as if he were caught in something beyond his control.

Bang! His gun exploded violently. And Hap . . . Hap's eyes continued to stare at him, full of terror and infinite sorrow, as the bullet rushed through the fog. . . .

Brrrriiiiingg!

What the hell was that? Will Dormer found himself standing in his motel room, a hammer in one hand, a nail in the other. For a moment, he didn't know what he was doing there. The telephone was ringing on his bedside table. He lifted the receiver and put it to his ear without saying anything. Someone was breathing on the other end. Then he heard the hateful voice of Walter Finch.

"This was always the worst time of night for me," Walter said quietly, his voice full of smarmy solicitude. "Too late for yesterday and too early for—"

"What is it?" Will demanded.

"I'm sorry about the tape. You'll get it back to-morrow, okay? I just know how hard this is for you and I have to be sure you'll follow through."

"I'll follow through."

"I've been thinking it over. I should tell them about Randy."

"I think that's a bad idea, Walter."

"But he's the patsy, Will, don't you see? And he *deserves* it. The things Kay told me about him. And how he'd bully her."

Will sighed. "These are cops, Walter, not children. You can't just drop it in their lap. Don't say anything about Randy, just come clean about your relationship with Kay. I can push them toward Randy when the time is right."

"But we don't have the gun, Will. How can we convince them he's guilty without that? Unless I tell them—"

"Did you keep the dress?" Will asked.

"The *dress*?"

"Kay's dress, her nail clippings. When you cleaned her, Walter, what did you do with those things?"

"You're right," Walter said after a moment. "That's even better than the murder weapon. We need to find a place where he could've taken the body."

"Well, where did *you* take her?" Will paused, but there was no answer from the other end. "She died in the cabin, right?"

"Yeah."

"But you took her somewhere else to clean her?"

Walter was evasive. "You don't want to think

about all that, Will. This is hard enough for you already."

"But it was an accident, right?"

"I didn't mean to kill her, Will. You understand that, don't you?"

"So what happened?"

The pause was so long from the other end that Will didn't think he was going to answer. But it's a lonely thing to be a killer, and Will knew that Finch needed to tell someone, to unburden himself. "She called me that night 'cause she'd fought with Randy. Wanted to talk. I told her to meet me at our place, the cabin at the beach. When she came, she was distraught and a little drunk. She told me that Randy and Tanya had been carrying on. I only wanted to comfort her. Hold her."

Will closed his eyes, imagining the scene.

"When I went to kiss her, she laughed. And she wouldn't stop," Walter went on. "You ever been laughed at, Will? I mean really laughed at? By someone you thought respected you? I just wanted to stop her from laughing. I hit her. Couple times. Just to stop her. Just to let her know. Randy did it all the time and she never left him, never even blamed him . . . but when *I* hit her, she started screaming. I tried to shut her up, but she was terrified, screaming her head off. I shook her and put my hand over her mouth and she was biting and screaming and I was scared, more scared than I've ever been. More scared than her. Then suddenly . . .

everything was clear. I'd gone so far, there was no turning back. After that, I was calm. So calm. You and I share a secret . . . we know how easy it is to kill someone. We know that ultimate taboo doesn't even exist outside our heads."

Walter didn't sound calm, nor did he sound easy. "But it wasn't murder." He expelled a long breath of air, like a tire going flat. "I didn't mean to kill her. It just ended up that way."

Will opened his eyes and glanced over to the torn photograph of Kay Connell that was propped against the base of the lamp on his bedside table. Kay alive, the wind blowing her hair, the awkward smile frozen forever on her lips.

"So where did you take her?" Will asked. It was hard to speak because his throat was so dry.

But Walter didn't rise to the bait. "Thank you for listening to me, Will. I feel a lot better talking about this stuff. I bet I'll sleep now. . . . Do you want to talk about Hap—"

Will slammed down the phone so hard the lamp nearly tumbled off the table. My God, what had he become? Making deals with a killer to save his own skin!

Furiously, he pulled the phone out of the wall. As though that would make Walter Finch disappear.

TWENTY-THREE

I n the morning, Will wandered out of the motel
lobby, thick with exhaustion, drunk with lack of
sleep. He was walking across the parking lot to the
Jeep when he saw Detective Ellie Burr waiting for
him. She was sitting on a low wall near the office
holding a silver necklace in her hand—Kay Connell's necklace, he presumed. She looked up and
smiled at him. Will felt a momentary panic. It was
as if she was . . . stalking him, almost. He forced
his lips to mutter good morning.

"Your phone isn't working," she said. "Fred
called that author. Said he was more than happy to
cooperate. We should go right there—he'll be in
first thing." Ellie stood from the wall, holding up
the necklace. "Forgot to tell you—they sell these

necklaces in a large chain of stores up in Anchorage. No way of finding out who bought it."

He nodded and began heading toward the Cherokee.

"I bet you're looking forward to going back to Los Angeles when this is all over," she said, speaking to his back.

Will stopped dead in his tracks. He turned to face her. There was something in Ellie's voice he didn't like. He studied her carefully, hoping he was mistaken. She was fiddling nervously with her backpack.

"Back to Robbery Homicide," she went on. "Or . . . maybe not."

"What are you saying, Ellie?"

She tried to smile, but she was ill at ease. "Nothing. You haven't been sleeping much, have you, Detective Dormer?"

"Not really," he admitted.

"Isn't that the difference between a good cop and a bad cop? A good cop can't sleep 'cause a piece of the puzzle's missing. A bad cop can't sleep 'cause his conscience won't let him." She held up the necklace for him to take. "You said that once."

Will stared at her, giving her a hard-eyed look he had used on countless suspects over the years, trying to break her down with sheer intimidation. But Ellie Burr—little innocent Ellie Burr—was not intimidated. She looked right back at him. He put out his hand and took the necklace from her.

"Sounds like something I'd say," he agreed.

The interrogation room was a narrow rectangle that was bare of unnecessary decoration. There were a small metal desk, three hard chairs, and a window looking out upon the station parking lot. It was a bleak place designed for people to confess their secrets. Will stood at the window, staring past the parking lot to a plume of white smoke that was drifting up into the mountains from the pulp mill factory. The smoke was hypnotic, like a prayer rising into the heavens. He blinked, forcing himself awake, and turned his attention back to the room.

Fred Duggar was asking questions, sitting across the table from Walter Finch. A tape recorder was running.

"You were acquainted with the deceased, Kay Connell?"

"Yes. Yes, I was." Walter was doing his best to be agreeable. His hair was combed and he wore a starched white shirt, sports jacket, and clean slacks, a portrait of a model citizen who wished only to be helpful. Ellie handed him a cup of coffee. "Thank you," he told her, the most polite killer you'd ever hope to meet.

Fred was trying to get a rhythm going with the questions, but he wasn't doing very well. "In what regard were you and her familiar?" he asked.

Will rolled his eyes. It was a badly phrased question and Walter seemed confused.

"How'd you know her, Finch?" Will tossed in.

Walter couldn't resist a smug smile. "She was a pretty avid reader of my detective novels."

"When did you meet her for the first time?" Fred asked.

"About a year ago. At one of my signings here in Nightmute. She hung around after, chatted to me about my writing. How she wanted to write. We got talking and she asked if she could visit me, to talk books and such."

"And she did?"

Walter nodded. "After a while we became quite close. She got comfortable enough to show me some of her own writing."

"What'd she write?" Will asked.

"Poetry actually."

"Any good?"

"No, not really."

"You tell her that?"

"No. Why should I?"

Will gave Finch his hard-eyed stare, the one he had used on Ellie Burr to little effect earlier in the morning.

"What, *exactly*, was the nature of your relationship, Finch?"

Walter seemed to consider this. "I think I was someone to talk to. Someone outside her everyday life. I think she needed that. I think that's why she first approached me."

"*Why'd* she need you for that?" Fred asked.

"Well . . . the boyfriend, Randy."

Will felt his body stiffen. For chrissake, Finch was going to fuck this up!

"Randy Stetz?" Ellie asked, for the benefit of the rolling tape recorder.

"Yes." Walter shook his head sadly, as if it was hard for a sensitive guy like himself to speak of such things. "He, uh . . . well, he hit her."

Will jumped into the conversation. "Finch, we know all this already."

"But it was getting worse," Walter said petulantly.

"So?"

"A lot worse. The frequency, the brutality."

Will leaned closer, putting his hands on the desk. "Why are you so eager to talk about Randy Stetz, Finch?"

Walter seemed to remember himself. "You're right. I'm sorry, Detective. It's hearsay, anyway, right? And I don't want to say anything that could be taken the wrong way."

Fred Duggar was clearly unhappy with Will for guiding the conversation away from Stetz. "Mr. Finch, firstly, anything you say to us at this stage is in strict confidence. Secondly, we're not a bunch of hotheads who're gonna draw all kinds of crazy conclusions."

Walter glanced with mild amusement from Will to Fred, as though wondering which one of the detectives he was supposed to believe.

"Carry on, please," Fred told him.

Walter pursed his lips. "I'm sure it's nothing . . . but Kay was getting scared." He looked down at his hands and sighed. "I suppose I have to take some of the blame . . ."

"Why's that?" Fred asked eagerly.

"Well, Randy knew about me. Not who I was . . . but he knew that she had a friend. Someone she confided in. It made him furious. She'd write to me about how scared of him she was. Her letters were getting more and more desperate."

"You don't still have them, by any chance?" Will asked, trying to keep any trace of sarcasm from his voice.

"I might," Walter answered pleasantly. "Do you think they'd help?"

"Perhaps." Will hovered over Walter, making his presence felt. "Anything else?"

Walter glanced to Fred for support. "Well, the thing that really worried her was the gun."

Will tensed. *The gun!* This was fucking unbelievable!

"He showed her this old handgun," Walter went on. "Wouldn't say where he got it. I mean, it wasn't his. Said he'd use it if he found out who she was seeing. . . ." Walter had been speaking to Fred, but he turned to Will. "Kept it hidden in the heating vent," he said, very deliberately. With relish. "You know, down in the skirting board."

Will felt dizzy. He moved away from Walter toward Fred, trying to think.

"Could be the thirty-eight," Fred said to him, excited.

Will kept his expression neutral. But inside he was fuming. It was bad enough to see Walter Finch go free, something else entirely to frame a teenage boy for a murder he hadn't committed.

Fred was energized. He got to his feet, flung open the door, and called out to Rich in the bull pen, "Get Judge Biggs on the phone!"

"What're you doing?" Will demanded.

"I'm gonna get a search warrant for Randy's place right now . . . got that?" he added, to Rich.

"I should get over there," Will said. He felt lost, hopelessly disoriented.

"Dormer, *you're* the guy he's talking to, for chrissake." Fred was incredulous. "Besides, we gotta wait for the warrant."

Will nodded. It was as if some giant wave were washing him along toward some perilously rocky shore. Through the glass door, he could see Rich picking up the phone in order to call Judge Biggs and get a search warrant.

Fred returned his attention to Walter. "When did Randy show her the gun?"

"Must've been . . . back in February. Or maybe even January."

A cold fury gripped hold of Will. Somehow he had to stop this. "Why didn't you come forward with all this when she died?" His voice was soft but dangerous.

"Kay swore me to secrecy. She didn't want anyone to know."

"Even when she was dead?"

"Well, I—"

"Beaten to death?" Will pressed.

"I respected her wishes—"

"Body dumped on a pile of trash?"

"I was her friend, so I—"

Will moved closer, in for the kill. "You weren't her friend!"

"An acquaintance, then," Walter said, flustered. "We were close and I—"

"She was an attractive girl. Did you have sex with her?"

"She was only seventeen."

"But attractive?"

"I suppose."

Will was relentless. He was aware that Fred and Ellie were watching him, uncomfortable with the venomous tone the interrogation was taking. But he didn't care.

"Did you have sex with her?" he repeated.

"I was a mentor to her," Walter answered, summoning his dignity.

"You gave her gifts."

"Sometimes."

"What kinds of gifts?"

"Books, mostly."

Will reached into his pocket and pulled out Kay's silver necklace. He threw it onto the table in front of Walter.

"You buy her this?"

Walter glanced at the necklace. Then looked up at Will. "Yes."

"*Why*? You liked the way it looked on her?"

"No, I—"

"Why else would you buy her jewelry?"

"It was just a present."

"Did you buy her dresses?"

"What's wrong with—"

"What kind of *mentor* were you?" Will shouted at him.

Walter was getting angry, too. "I gave her things she couldn't have!"

Will grabbed Walter by the lapels of his sports jacket and pulled him to his feet.

"You just wanted to fuck her!"

Will felt Fred taking hold of his arm. "Dormer, come on. Come on," Fred said, pulling him away to the far side of the room. "You need to go cool down, okay?"

Will nodded. He knew he was out of control. He stepped out of the interrogation room and stood by the water cooler, just breathing and trying to get a grip on himself.

What the hell am I going to do? If he went along

with this, if he let Walter Finch frame a teenage kid
for murder, he knew he might just as well put his
gun in his mouth and pull the trigger. He had become a bad cop, but not that bad. He had to think.
Was there *any* way to make this work out right?
Keep an innocent shithead of a kid from spending
the rest of his life in prison, get the real perp behind bars, and still save his own ass?

From back in the room, he could hear Fred
speaking. "Mr. Finch, I have to apologize for my
colleague. He's been under a lot of pressure. He's
a good cop."

Walter giggled. "I'd hate to see the bad cop!"

Will Dormer shook his head. Good cop, bad
cop—for Will, these had once been firm principles
to steer by. But not anymore. They had become
gradually blurred so he didn't know which end
was up.

But at least he had an idea what he might do . . .
if there was still enough time.

Troubled, Ellie Burr peered out from the interrogation room window to the parking lot outside.
She watched Will rush from the building, jog over
to the Cherokee, and fire up the engine. The tires
squealed and the Jeep lurched out of the lot in a
cloud of blue-white exhaust. She knew something
was *very* wrong here, though she still didn't completely have the nerve to name it.

Good cop, bad cop . . .

From the bull pen, she heard Rich slam down the phone. "We got our warrant!" Rich's voice was triumphant. The case was breaking, moving fast, carrying them all along.

Finch stood up from the desk with a subtle know-it-all smile. A strange man. She didn't much like him. But he had been helpful, she had to admit. Fred Duggar was certainly pleased with the author. He pumped Walter's hand. "Thank you, Mr. Finch!" he said excitedly. She watched as Fred raced out from the station, eager to serve Randy Stetz with the warrant. Fred had always said that the killer was Randy, from the very start, so this was his vindication.

Everyone was in motion except Ellie, who was gnawed with a feeling of uneasiness.

"You're not going?" Walter asked her.

She shook her head. Finch followed her out of the building, trying his best to be friendly. He wanted to share some cop-talk. As if he was one of them, on the inside, just because he wrote detective novels.

"Aren't you all on the Connell case?"

"I'm covering the shooting of Detective Dormer's partner," she answered.

"I heard about that. Tragic."

"Yes, it was," she agreed. "Good-bye, Mr. Finch."

Standing in the parking lot, Ellie watched Fred's squad car peel out of the gate onto the street, taking

the same direction in which Will Dormer had gone
a few minutes earlier. She began walking to her
pickup truck. But Walter called after her.

"If you're on a different case, should I still be
calling *you* about those letters of Kay's?"

Ellie nodded distractedly, eager to get away.
Finch was really creepy, somehow. She climbed
into the cab of her truck wondering why she was
suddenly so depressed. She had always imagined
a world of good and evil, light and dark, where
you were a warrior for either one side or the
other—it was what had made her want to be a police detective. But at the moment, everything
seemed to her only a blurred, confusing shade of
gray.

TWENTY-FOUR

Will Dormer drove recklessly through town, knowing that time was against him. He skidded around a corner and raced down a side street until he came to an old wood-framed building where Randy Stetz lived in an apartment above his grandfather's garage.

He pulled into the alley behind the garage and leaped from the Jeep without bothering to park properly. There was a chain-link fence he needed to jump, which slowed him down. Once he was over, he ran across a shabby patch of backyard and went up the outside steps to Randy's apartment two stairs at a time. He came to a landing and remembered only just in time to put on a pair of latex gloves so he wouldn't leave his own prints behind. Will was certain that Finch had planted the .38 Smith & Wesson in the teenager's apartment. Somehow he had to find the gun and get out before Fred Duggar arrived with his court search warrant.

The front door was his first obstacle. Will performed his credit card trick, but precious seconds ticked by, nearly a minute. His hand wasn't completely steady. *Come on, come on!* He was starting to panic when the lock finally slipped open. With relief, he stepped inside the darkened room and tried to take it in all at once. The apartment was depressing, a joyless, dysfunctional clutter. There was a stack of *Hustler* magazines on a cheap coffee table by a tattered sofa. Ashtrays that needed dumping. A film of dust on every surface. Will could see a narrow bedroom through an open door. There was a motorcycle in the corner, halfway disassembled with parts scattered on the floor. An unmade bed that looked as though the sheets had never been changed. A torn blind on the window, yellow with age.

Will absorbed the apartment in a frantic second, then set to work. He began with the heating vent, yanking off the grille. The gun wasn't there. *Fuck!* He looked about, trying to put himself into Finch's mind—Walter pretending to be Randy Stetz. The hiding place couldn't be too obvious, but at the same time, Walter *wanted* the gun to be found, so it shouldn't be too hard either. But where? Will walked into the bedroom and pulled the bed from the wall. He felt along all four sides of the mattress. Nothing. He shoved the bed back into place and turned to the bureau, yanking open the drawers. He felt furiously through the clothes, socks, underwear, and T-shirts. But there was no gun.

Will turned in a circle, his eyes searching. He walked back into the living room, crossing to a trunk that was piled high with junk. He raked all the stuff onto the floor, then began rummaging through the trunk. The trunk was full of papers and magazines but no .38 Smith & Wesson. *Think!* Fred Duggar probably had his search warrant and was heading over. Will threw everything back inside the trunk and piled up the mess more or less where it had been.

Kneeling on the living room floor, he saw a toolbox he had missed next to the motorcycle. This had to be it! Will raced back into the bedroom and began pulling out oil-covered tools, wrenches and sockets and screwdrivers. But still no gun. Will was throwing the tools back into the box when he heard a squad car skid up outside, its doors flying open. He leaped to his feet and peered out through a narrow slit in the window blind. Three cops were spilling out of the car—Fred Duggar and two uniforms, Rich and Francis. Will still had a few more seconds. He went to the closet and began feeling for a bulky weight in the hanging clothes. *Nothing!*

There were footsteps climbing the outside stairs. There came a loud knocking at the door.

"Stetz!" It was Fred Duggar's voice, full of lawful authority.

Will rushed to a shelf by the bed. His hands fluttered over the ashtray, a pile of comic books, an empty shoe box.

"We're coming in!" Fred bellowed from outside.

Will was setting the shoe box back on the shelf when the front door shuddered loudly. The cops on the landing were ramming the door with their shoulders. Will stepped from the bedroom, his eyes darting about. He saw an open door to the bathroom. Quickly he slipped inside the bathroom and closed the door behind him. The bathroom was basic and wasn't going to win any *Good Housekeeping* award: a filthy toilet, a sink, a narrow tub, a window with frosted glass, everything covered with grit and old soap scum. It was the window that had led him here, a brief flicker of hope. But he soon saw it was too small for him to escape through.

From the next room, he heard a crack as the front door shattered open. The three cops tumbled into the apartment, excited and full of adrenaline.

"Turn the place over!" Fred shouted, enjoying himself during a fine opportunity for violence.

Will was trapped, no exit, no hope. He flattened himself against the bathroom wall wondering what the hell he was going to say to explain himself. The way he was positioned, the bathroom door would hide him when it opened, but that would be only a brief reprieve. He listened as the cops searched roughly through Randy's stuff, going through the same places where Will had already looked, yanking at bureau drawers, pulling the bed out from the wall. He saw a shadow beneath the door, two feet. He waited, frozen, not daring to breathe. The door handle began to turn. . . .

"Got it!" Rich cried.

The feet moved away from the bathroom and Will exhaled. From the sounds he heard, all three cops had gone into Randy's bedroom. Will opened the bathroom door carefully, just a crack. Fred, Rich, and Francis were in the bedroom, their backs to him, gathered around the motorcycle in the corner.

It was the only opportunity Will was going to get. Silently, he slipped out of the bathroom and came up behind them, pretending he had just arrived.

Fred saw him first, glancing over his shoulder. "Just in time, Dormer."

Rich held up the .38 Smith & Wesson, dripping with oil. "Had it in a can of motor oil."

Will felt like kicking himself. *A can of motor oil!* If he had only had a few minutes more time . . .

"What the fuck is this?" a voice called angrily, coming in through the broken front door. The three cops and Will turned to face the new arrival.

It was Randy Stetz, and he wasn't happy.

*   *   *

Detective Ellie Dormer was having a very different afternoon, tranquil and pensive, climbing over the rocks on the beach in front of the old fishing cabin. She wasn't sure what had brought her there again, except maybe the hope that some new insight might come to her if she was in the place where Hap Eckhart had died.

She made her way past the rock where Farrell had been wounded and climbed slowly down to the water. It was a perfect summer afternoon, hardly any wind, and she enjoyed the quiet of being alone. Waves lapped gently against the rocky shore, ebbing in and out with a peaceful sucking sound. Gulls called overhead. As an adolescent, Ellie had spent many hours by herself on such beaches, dreaming her dreams, planning her future. She had made her dreams come true. There she was, an honest-to-God detective. Only it had turned out to be a more complicated profession than she had ever imagined.

Ellie was wandering along the waterline, not consciously thinking about the case, when she saw something glittering, a small object that had been caught between two rocks. Curious, she stopped and checked more closely. It looked like gold, or more likely brass. A penny? As a kid, Ellie had been a serious scavenger, picking up all sorts of interesting things on the beach. She stooped over,

reached with her fingers between the two rocks,
and pulled the glittering thing out.

It was a bullet casing! A fired shell that had been
ejected from a gun.

She frowned, holding it close to her face. The
shell was not a .38 or a .45—she could tell that
much immediately from her own familiarity with
these calibers.

What was it then? Nine millimeter, maybe? It
probably had come from an automatic, not a revolver, unless someone had stopped to empty the
chambers of his cylinder, perhaps to reload. But
this did not fit with the events of the evening when
Hap Eckhart had been killed.

It *was* a 9mm shell—she was almost certain.
Ellie's frown deepened, remembering something.
She slipped the shell casing into her pocket and
climbed quickly back over the rocks away from the
beach to the road where she had left her pickup.
Ellie drove home, hurried upstairs to her bedroom,
and flung open her closet door. It was a good thing
she never threw stuff out. She got on her knees and
burrowed past her shoes to a stack of boxes at the
rear of the closet. The box she wanted was close to
the bottom, marked ACAD on top with a black pen.
She pulled it out onto the floor of her bedroom.

Ellie began pulling out papers and class sched-
ules and handbooks from her years as a student at
the police academy. Everything brought back
memories. An examination where she had scored a

perfect 100. A ribbon she had won on the firing range. A note from a professor of criminal justice on whom she'd had a major crush. Then she found what she'd been looking for: a term paper she'd done her last year. The cover was just as she remembered it: "Securing the Crime Scene: The Leland Street Murders" by Eleanor P. Burr.

How proud she'd been of this report at the time! It seemed ancient history now, but maybe it would still be useful. Sitting on the floor by the open box, Ellie opened the report to the middle and began quickly scanning pages. A few minutes later, she spotted what she was looking for, a single phrase three-quarters of the way down a page:

. . . Detective Dormer's backup weapon, a Walther 9mm, to immobilize Langley . . .

Ellie closed her eyes and sighed. Her heart was pounding.

TWENTY-FIVE

Will watched Fred Duggar and Rich work on Randy Stetz. He felt sick at heart, rotten clear to the soul. He wanted to scream the kid's innocence, but he said nothing. He leaned against a desk in the bull pen with Chief Nyback alongside him. From where they were positioned, they could see through the glass door into the interrogation room, but they couldn't hear the questioning. Randy was seated at the small metal desk with handcuffs on his wrists. He looked sullen and scared.

Will tried to tell himself that Randy deserved what he was getting. The kid had beaten up Kay Connell. When you were that bad at the age of seventeen, the future only offered more opportunity for trouble. Randy was surely going to end up in prison one day . . . so why not now?

"We can get you on a flight first thing tomorrow," Charlie said.

Will nodded. It would be great to get the hell out of Nightmute, Alaska. But he felt no joy.

"Sure I can't talk you into staying a couple of days?" the chief asked. "Show you what else goes on around here."

It made it worse for Will, what a decent guy Charlie Nyback was. He didn't dare look the chief in the eye. "I have to get back," he muttered. He nodded toward Fred through the glass. "Nightmute's finest can take it from here."

Charlie cleared his throat awkwardly. Will sensed a speech was coming.

"Will, thank you for coming up here. I know things . . . well, we wouldn't have got him without you."

"No?"

"No. We'd already moved on. It's thanks to you—you and Hap—that we came back to Stetz."

The irony was unbearable. Just then the door to the interrogation room opened and Fred swaggered out, looking like God's gift to law enforcement.

"Now he's saying he was with Tanya Francke the night Kay was killed," Fred told them with a smirk.

"That's what she told me," Will agreed.

Fred turned angrily to Will. "When?"

"I questioned her the other day. She told me in confidence. Didn't want anyone to know."

"Planning on telling anyone?"

"I'm telling you, aren't I? I wasn't interested in Randy, anyway."

Fred gave Will a look of withering disdain, then turned his attention to the chief. "Randy and Tanya were screwing around on Kay. It's pretty clear she's just trying to protect him."

"What's he saying about the gun?" Nyback asked.

"Says it isn't his. But once we've got the ballistics match he's gonna start being a little more forthcoming. . . . You're leaving?" Fred asked, turning back to Will. He did not seem overly saddened by the idea.

"First thing tomorrow," the chief said, answering for Will.

Fred grinned. "If Spencer's not too hungover for flying."

Nyback chuckled. In Alaska, drinking was apparently still considered a manly virtue.

Fred looked at Will. "They drink beer down in L.A.?" he asked.

It was, Will supposed, as close to an offer of friendship as Detective Fred Duggar was ever going to make. Fred was in a mood to celebrate and perform the ancient cop ritual of brewski and bullshit. And why not? Fred was the detective of

the hour, a major dude. It was just a pity his success came at the wrong guy's expense.

The bar where they went that night was a
shanty on the edge of town near the water, a dive
with plenty of atmosphere. There were five or six
cops seated around a long, beer-soaked table. Farrell had come to the party, recovered from his
wound, along with Fred, Francis, Rich, and a few
others whose names Will didn't know or care to
know.

Music thumped on the jukebox, sad country
songs about cheating and other failures. Across the
bar, a group of men were gathered around a green
velvet table beneath a smoky lamp. To Will, the
click-clack of their pool balls mixed with the country music and the smell of beer. It all seemed hopeless, a tapestry of despair. He wished at that
moment that he hadn't come tonight, but not coming would have made him stand out—a tactical
mistake under the circumstances. Besides, he was
just as anxious to get drunk as the next man,
maybe more so. One of the cops whose name he
didn't know arrived from the bar with a tray of
mugs full of dark beer. Will grabbed one. It was far
from his first tonight.

"I can't believe it. Randy Stetz!" Farrell was saying. His friends had been filling him in on events,
everything he had missed while he was laid up in
the hospital. "He was an asshole."

"Didn't you know him when he was a little kid?" Fred asked one of the officers Will didn't know. A young guy with a lean face.

"Our dads were on the same boat," the cop answered. "We used to wait for them together."

"Just a bad seed, huh?" This from Fred.

Francis turned to Will. "How do you like our beer?"

Will slammed down his empty glass and squeezed his eyes shut. "I like it fine," he answered.

"What Detective Dormer needs is a little shut-eye," Fred told the others.

"White nights been hard on you?" Rich asked.

Will smiled. "Haven't been easy."

"Better than winter." Farrell laughed.

"In winter the sun barely comes up for five straight months," Rich said.

"Like being swallowed up in a black hole," Fred said.

Frankly, a black hole didn't sound half bad to Will. No more midnight sun. He felt the presence of someone coming up behind him.

"Hi, guys," said a girlish voice. Ellie Burr was joining them.

"Nancy Drew!" Fred called out happily. "Pull up a seat!"

"You hear?" Francis asked. "We got him."

"Rich found the gun," Farrell told her. And Farrell hadn't even been there.

"I heard," Ellie said, grabbing a chair from the next table.

Fred was eyeing her, a big grin on his face. "Something's on Nancy's mind."

Ellie reached into her vest pocket and pulled out a Ziploc bag with the shell casing inside. "Found this out on the beach."

"What is it?" Farrell peered drunkenly at the bag.

"Shell casing." She paused, looking at Will. "Nine millimeter."

Will felt his insides contract with tension. Ellie was looking at him, studying his reaction. "The murder weapon was a thirty-eight," she added. "And none of us carries a nine-millimeter duty weapon . . . or backup weapon? Right?"

Rich threw a handful of peanut shells at her. "Get a hobby, would ya?"

Ellie brushed off the shells without moving her eyes from Will. "It's a legitimate point, isn't it, Detective Dormer?"

Everyone seemed to turn his way, their faces spinning in Will's exhausted vision. "The case is closed, Ellie," he told her, standing up unsteadily from the table. "I got the next round."

He headed in the direction of the bar, weaving his way through the smoke and music and laughter. A good thing everyone was drunk tonight, himself included. *What does a 9mm shell mean? By itself, nothing.* Tomorrow he was going to get the hell out of there. But tonight . . . tonight he felt as if he were being slowly suffocated by this town, this case.

He stood at the bar, waving a twenty at the bartender, knowing that Ellie Burr was watching his every move.

The night spun on, with plenty of beer and laughter. And Ellie watching, never taking her eyes from him. It was late when they finally spilled out the front door into the parking lot. Will looked up at the night sky overhead with a dismay that was close to terror. The sky was white, glowing with terribly unnatural light.

Fred slapped Will on the shoulder. With enough beer, they were best pals. "It's been something, Dormer!"

Ellie came up to him, her turn to say good-bye. To Will's astonishment, she threw her arms around him in a kind of California hug—the sort of thing movie people, and flaky New Agers, did but he would not have suspected Ellie of such an impulse. Will didn't know what to do with his hands, whether he was supposed to hug her in return. He didn't think so.

"Working with you has been amazing," she told him.

He felt her hands moving down to the small of his back, until they came to the bump of his holster. His backup 9mm. Abruptly she moved from his embrace, recoiling, stumbling backward. Her cheeks were burning. Will stared at her, but for the first time all night, she refused to look back. She was ashamed.

True to form, Fred was oblivious. "You gonna run Will to the airport?" he asked Ellie, still thinking they were all the best of chums.

"No, I have to go pick up those letters. Detective Dormer can just leave the Jeep out at the airport"—awkwardly, she forced herself to look at him—"if that's okay?"

Will was overcome with shame. This was a special hell he hadn't realized was in store for him tonight: disillusioning a young woman who had believed in him.

"That's fine," he mumbled.

Farrell stumbled against Rich, the two of them very drunk. "Get some sleep!" he called out good-naturedly.

Wouldn't that be nice? Will thought. But he didn't think he would.

TWENTY-SIX

The night wasn't over yet. Will Dormer had an appointment to keep.

He drove the Cherokee to the Mariners' Monument at the foot of the harbor, near where he and Hap had landed in the floatplane what seemed like several lifetimes ago. He stepped out of the car into the fresh air, strangely sober after all he'd had to drink. It was the memory of Ellie's face that had sobered him, her disillusioned eyes, like a slap in the face.

Walter Finch was waiting, sitting on a bench at the foot of the memorial to Nightmute's drowned sailors, staring out to sea. Will crossed over to him.

"I really thought you wanted to kill me in that interview room," Finch said mildly.

"I did."

Walter giggled. As if the idea of Will wanting to kill him was funny somehow.

"Randy Stetz is in jail," Will said pointedly.

"Told you I could write an ending they'd like. You're too wrapped up in the details."

"He's *innocent*."

"No, he isn't. He beat Kay. And one day he'd have done something worse. Maybe a lot worse. You know that, they know that. That's why they're happy to see him in the frame." Walter cocked his head coyly. "So when were you going to point them at me, Will? When you found out where Kay's dress was? Where I took the body? Right? If you had the gun and the forensics it wouldn't matter what crazy bullshit I said about you killing your partner, would it?"

Will stared at him bleakly. "How'd you know I planted the gun?"

"You're a good man, Will. I know that, even if you've forgotten it. You agreed to help me before I'd even shown you the tape recorder. You *had* to have a wild card."

Will held out his hand. "The tape."

After a moment's hesitation, Walter shrugged and pulled a minicassette tape from his pocket. Will grabbed it from his hand violently and cracked the plastic case in two. He ripped out the ribbon of brown tape and hurled it into the sea. When the tape was destroyed, he turned his fury on Walter, whirling around and rushing at him. Walter tried to get away, but he wasn't fast enough. Will slammed him against a concrete pilaster.

"Did you make copies?"

Walter stared up into Will's bloodshot eyes. "You go from calm to rage in the blink of an eye—you know that? But that's okay, so do I. Kay used to tease me about it—"

Will grabbed Walter's throat, choking off the words.

"*Did you make copies?*"

Walter shook his head. "Why would I?" he managed hoarsely.

"To stop me turning you in . . . or killing you."

"I don't have any hold over you, Will. I never did. You made your own choices. I might as well not exist. And why would you kill me? It wouldn't help Randy. And after your scene at the police station, I don't think it's gonna be good for you if I turn up dead."

"Doesn't have to be murder."

Walter almost seemed to be enjoying himself. "An accident, huh? Like Hap. Like Kay."

"It took at least ten minutes to beat Kay Connell to death!" Will hissed furiously. "Some accident. *Ten fucking minutes!*"

"And it only took you a fraction of a second to kill your partner, but it doesn't make it any more of an accident, Will, does it?"

Will was dizzy with rage and frustration. His hand tightened on Walter's throat, while his other hand brought his gun up to the writer's temple. "Is this an accident?"

"If you want it to be," Walter gasped.

The writer's face was turning red. Yet incredibly, he smiled. He wasn't afraid. It made Will positively ballistic. He could hear the waves crashing behind him, a sound echoing his anger. His fingers squeezed at Walter's throat, tightening his grip. But still the writer smiled. He seemed to know something about Will that Will himself didn't know.

He let go suddenly, sickened at his own behavior. He shoved Finch aside, resigned. The writer stumbled backward against the monument, coughing and wheezing for breath.

"It's over, Walter," he told him. "I'm telling them everything. About Hap. About you. Everything."

Walter seemed genuinely bemused. "What good is that going to do?"

"It's going to end this."

Walter shook his head patiently, as if he was dealing with a backward child. "You haven't been sleeping, Will. You're not thinking straight. Not seeing what's going on around you. You *shot* your partner. Then you *lied* about it. It would be my word against yours. Don't you see? You're a killer. You're a liar. You're *tainted*. Forever. You don't get to choose when to tell the truth, Will. The truth's supposed to be beyond that." He gestured to the waves. "And that tape was the only physical proof that we've ever spoken outside of that interview room."

Will froze. *It was true!* Without the tape he had no proof, nothing, only a crazy story that no one would believe. Great cop that he was, he hadn't thought of this when he threw the cassette tape into the water. Will's knees felt weak. He had to grab on to the pilaster for support.

"To them I'm just a writer Kay looked up to," Walter was saying, his voice unbearably calm. "Randy Stetz is the killer. And you're the hero cop. Things are as they should be. Your life's work intact. An abusive scumbag in jail." He put his hand on Will's shoulder. "Go back to Los Angeles, Will."

Will jerked his shoulder away violently.

Walter only smiled. "The case against Randy is solid enough," he said. "And I'll take care of everything else up here. I've got it all worked out."

Will stared at Walter Finch in mute disbelief, wondering how such a smarmy little killer, a crime writer, had been able to manipulate him from start to finish. It was intolerable. Even if Will confessed the truth to Nyback, Finch would in all probability still go free. Will sensed that, if he could only think his way through, there must be a solution. But he couldn't think. His mind churned sluggishly. He was drained and exhausted.

Walter fixed him with a condescending smile. "This is your sixth night, Will," he said, full of concern. "You broke my record."

Will drove back to the Pioneer Lodge, set his bag on the bed in his room, and began throwing his clothes in. A few hours later, he would be on a floatplane to Anchorage, then on a big jet to Los Angeles. He tried to tell himself that things would be better once he was back in L.A., but he knew this was only one more lie. Like Humpty Dumpty, he had taken a major tumble, and there was nothing that was ever going to put his life back together again.

Suddenly he was certain that someone was in the room with him. He wheeled around and . . . fuck! *There was Hap, sitting in a dark corner watching him pack!* Will breathed in and out, steadying himself. *Whew!* This lack of sleep was getting scary. Six nights. A record! Cagily, he ignored the hallucination, turning back to his suitcase. The thing to do, obviously, was take this slowly, one step at a time. He scooped his underwear and socks out of a drawer and put them in the case, arranging them carefully. Next he went to the closet. He pulled out the shirt he had been wearing the night he killed Hap. There was still blood on the sleeve. Ruthlessly, he stuffed it in the suitcase, blood and all. Then came the wrinkled, filthy suit he'd been wearing the afternoon he'd gone swimming in the icy river full of logs.

Finally, there came the question of weapons. What he would carry on the plane tomorrow? With a sigh, and remembering Ellie Burr's disillusionment, he unstrapped the holster from the back of his belt and threw the 9mm Walther into his bag. His backup gun hadn't done him a whole lot of good in Alaska and by sending it with his luggage he would be able to cut down on paperwork at the airport. Frankly, he'd just as soon never see the damn 9mm again.

Will was doing all right, just packing his suitcase, taking one thing at a time. Except Hap was still sitting in the corner of the room, watching him pack. And then the phone rang. Hadn't he pulled the cord out last night? *How could it be fucking ringing?* A small thing, but it sent him over the top . . . one little thing too many, piled up on all the other little things. He threw the phone violently across the room, cord and all, sending it thumping against the blanket he'd nailed over the window. The force of the phone brought the blanket halfway down, flooding the motel room with an unbearable glow.

Light! He had to squint, it was so bright. This was the last straw—it really was. He set to work plugging the hole. He pulled a large dresser from the wall—an armoire, he supposed—dragged it across the room, and set it against the window. It helped cut down the glow, but not nearly enough. Light was still getting in. He rolled up a blanket from the bed and stuffed it into the crack between the armoire and the window. Next came three pillows. But no matter what he added, the light still came pouring into the room, burning his eyes. He was looking about wildly for magazines, towels, anything to plug the hole, when there came a sudden knocking on his door.

Will flung open the door to find Rachel standing in the hall. She stumbled backward, startled by his appearance.

"Detective Dormer. Will . . . I . . ." Words failed her. She could only stare at him with concern.

"What is it?"

"Someone was complaining about the noise. Says he can't sleep."

Couldn't sleep? Now this was funny! The irony was profound. Will started laughing. *He* was keeping someone from sleeping! It just got funnier and funnier, the more he thought about it. Rachel looked past him at the mess in the room, becoming more alarmed.

"Shhh!" she told him. "Shhh . . ."

She turned him back into the room and closed the door behind them.

"Will, what's wrong?"

"It's so fucking bright!" he complained. He was already back at work, wadding up balls of newspaper to stuff into the crack between the armoire and the window, where light was seeping in.

Rachel caught hold of his arm. "Will, it's pitch-black in here."

Was she blind? He pointed to the beam of light that was shining like a searchlight through a crack he hadn't managed to stop up. It was an insidious crack—tiny, yes, but terrible. The kind of crack that kept a person from sleeping six nights in a row!

Rachel went to the light switch and flipped on the current. The lamp on the bedside table exploded with light that nearly knocked him off his feet. Will blinked, his senses overwhelmed. But he saw that she was right. If a sixty-watt bulb could dazzle his eyes, the room had been very dark indeed. He turned back toward his handiwork at the window and groaned, suddenly understanding how crazy he had become.

"Please. Turn it off," he told her in a small voice.

Working in the dark, Rachel helped him drag the armoire away from the window back to its proper position against the wall. Then she cleaned the assortment of pillows, blankets, and wadded-up paper.

Will watched as she tidied his room, grateful for her help. There was no doubt about the fact that Rachel Clement was an unusually kind

woman. He felt an odd intimacy with her in that
darkened room. Not sexual, not after six sleepless
nights. But to his surprise, he found himself
telling her things he had never told anybody before, about what had happened in L.A., the child-
killer who had caused him to cross the line from
good cop to bad.

"There's this guy, Wayne Dobbs," he began.
"Twenty-four, works part-time at a copy store.
And every morning he watches an eight-year-old
boy waiting for his car pool 'cross the street."

Rachel nodded, encouraging him to continue.
As she cleared the window of debris, a natural
light from outside gradually sifted into the
room—a pleasant light that chased away the
nightmarish shadows.

Will went on with his story. "Six months he
watches, till one day he gets up the guts to go out
there and grab that boy before the car pool comes.
Dobbs keeps the boy in his apartment for three
days. Tortures him. Makes him do things . . ."

Rachel stopped folding a blanket. She listened,
half turned from him, horrified.

"Finally, he's had enough. Gets a rope and
hangs the boy in an unused storage space in the
basement of the building. But he didn't do it right.
The little boy's neck didn't break, and he died
from shock. Landlord found him five days later."

"One of your cases?" Rachel asked uneasily.

"Me and Hap. A year and a half ago. I knew the

second I met Dobbs that he was guilty. That's my job. That's what I do. I assign guilt. Any cop tells you otherwise is talking to a camera. Find the evidence. Figure out who did it. Put them away. Only this time there isn't enough. Reasonable doubt to a jury, 'cause a jury's never met a child-killer before. But I have."

Will paused, remembering what he'd done, the line he had crossed. "I took blood samples from the boy's body and planted them in Dobbs's apartment. Arrested him the next day."

He watched Rachel's face, searching for judgment. But she kept her face absolutely still. He couldn't tell what she was thinking.

"I'd never done anything like that before. . . . It's funny. I *knew* . . . right when I did it that it was gonna catch up with me. I'm just not that guy, you know? I mean, it's one thing to think about it . . . to know it *needs* to be done. It's a whole other thing to actually do it. But Dobbs *was* guilty. And Dobbs needed to be convicted. End justifies means, right?"

She turned to him. "How did it catch up to you?"

"Internal Affairs is coming down on our department. Hap was gonna cut a deal, bring me straight into it. Dobbs would've been one of the first cases they reopened . . . but now that's not gonna happen. I don't know how to feel about that."

He came to a stop. There wasn't anything more to tell. "Do you think it's wrong, what I did?"

"I'm not in any position to judge," she answered, looking away.

"Why not?"

Rachel didn't answer immediately. "There's two kinds of people live in Alaska—those born here, and those who came here to escape from somewhere else. . . . I wasn't born here."

"But what do you *think*?"

Her eyes were soft with the gentle early-morning light of a new summer day. "I guess it's about what you think is right at the time," she told him quietly, "and what you're willing to live with."

Later, Rachel fell asleep on his bed, fully dressed. He hadn't touched her physically, though what had happened between them seemed almost more intimate than sex. She had saved him. Just talking to Rachel, telling her the truth, had made him clear. It was like a shadow had lifted from his life, all the confusion and doubt, and Will Dormer knew without question what he had to do.

He showered and shaved and put on a clean suit. There wasn't enough sleep in the universe to make up for all the sleep he had missed. Nevertheless, he was more solid than he had felt for a long time. He pulled out the author photograph he had of Walter Finch standing in front of a lake and a mountain glacier. He folded the photo, stuck it in his pocket, and turned one more time to look at Rachel sleeping on his bed. She was beautiful. There was no doubt about it.

Will was about to leave the room when he remembered one final item. He picked up the gold badge, his Los Angeles detective shield, from the top of the bureau and clipped it to his belt.

TWENTY-SEVEN

Ellie Burr didn't know what to do with herself. After she left the male-bonding beer bash at the bar, she went home but found herself unable to snatch more than a few hours' sleep. This was unheard of for Ellie, to have trouble sleeping. She rose early and drove over to the Pioneer Lodge, where she parked and sat in her pickup outside Will Dormer's darkened window, meditating on her choices.

Should she take the 9mm shell she'd found on the beach to Chief Nyback and lay out her suspicions? The chief could stop Dormer from flying back to California while they investigated further. Of course, it would be a huge step to accuse such a respected cop as Will Dormer of deliberately shooting his own partner. Ellie wasn't certain she had enough evidence. She was only a novice detective after all, brand-new at this. Meanwhile, if she was wrong—if the markings on the 9mm shell *didn't* match Dormer's backup gun—it would be hugely embarrassing. In fact, this was something that could hurt her career, not to mention the chance of any of the guys at the department ever taking her seriously again. And if the ballistics *did* match, what did that really prove? Hap Eckhart had been killed, after all, with a .38. That was the confusing part of all this, shredding her theory.

The more she thought it over, Ellie realized she simply didn't have the hard evidence she needed. She had no choice but to let Dormer go home. Meanwhile, she thought she might as well pick up Kay's letters today from Walter Finch—he had told her he'd be at his Lake Kgun house, if she didn't mind the drive, or he could bring them into the station next week.

Ellie started up her truck, glancing one more time at Will Dormer's window. She remembered the way he had looked at her last night outside the bar, his bloodshot eyes full of shame and guilt. Damn it, she was *certain* she was right! Dormer had the motive, the opportunity, and a 9mm Walther in a holster in the small of his back. But Eckhart had been killed with the wrong gun . . . and there was nothing she could do about that. It was frustrating, but she had to let it go. Will Dormer would remain unfinished business, a nagging doubt that justice had not been served. Ellie suspected that this was the sort of thing that made cops cynical, watching year after year as bad guys got away.

It was a gloomy morning, matching her mood. Ellie pulled out of the parking lot and headed to Lake Kgun to see Walter Finch, certain that she would never have an opportunity to solve any important crime.

Ellie headed inland over a treacherous mountain highway of blind curves and cliffs that dropped off into stomach-lurching vistas. She drove at the speed limit and occasionally an impatient car behind her passed dangerously. Alaskan drivers were famous for their daredevil stunts—it was part of life on the Last Frontier. Once or twice, Ellie was tempted to pull someone over until she could summon a local cop to hand out a ticket—she had a revolving police light in her glove compartment that she could stick on top of her cab. But she wasn't in the mood to play traffic cop, so she let them go. It occurred to her that a year ago she would have pursued *any* crime, no matter how small. Maybe this was the start of "going wrong"—a long, slow slide until one day you woke up to find you were the object of an Internal Affairs probe. . . .

The drive took Ellie nearly an hour and a half. At last the highway came over a rise and she saw

Lake Kgun below her, steel-gray beneath a glowering sky. A storm was coming. It was an impressive sight, a mountain lake with a glacier rising up steeply into storm clouds, but Ellie was not much in the mood for sights. She drove through the sleepy tourist town, consulted the address Finch had given her, and found his summer retreat twenty minutes later.

It was a large ramshackle wooden house directly on the lake with a boathouse and a private dock and a spectacular view of the mountains. Probably it had been very nice there years ago, but now the house was falling apart, with plastic sheeting covering the windows instead of glass. The entire rear of the building appeared to be a construction zone, but it looked as though Finch had run out of money at some point and the repairs had been long abandoned. Still, Ellie imagined this was the sort of inspiring locale that writers were always seeking in order to create their imaginary worlds.

She parked in the dirt turnout alongside the main house and walked up a path to the front door. Finch opened the door before she reached it. He was wearing a dark sweater and slacks and somehow *looked* like her idea of a writer—he seemed a little odd, maybe, but probably you needed to be eccentric to succeed in such a profession.

He was delighted to see her. "Detective Burr! Didn't expect you so soon!"

She followed him inside, declining an offer of coffee and a sandwich, saying she needed to pick up the letters and get back to Nightmute as soon as possible. The interior of the house was big and drafty and sparsely furnished. He led her up a flight of creaky stairs to the second floor, where he said he had his office.

"You think these could really strengthen the case against Randy?" He seemed eager to discuss police matters.

She shrugged, not wanting to get into details. His office was a small room with a slanted ceiling. The plastic tacked over the window was crackling in the wind. It was hard for Ellie to imagine any-one working in such a bleak and lonely room. There was something . . . she couldn't quite put her finger on it . . . something *really* creepy about Walter Finch and his Lake Kgun home.

Walter crossed to a chest of drawers. "They're in here, somewhere," he told her vaguely, pulling out a drawer.

Ellie wandered over to his typewriter. She'd al-ways heard that writers worked on computers these days, but Finch was clearly an exception. There was a piece of paper spooled through the roller, a title page. *The Blink of an Eye* by Walter Finch.

"Starting a new book, Mr. Finch?"

He turned and nodded.

She felt a surge of anxiety. He smiled at her pleasantly, but . . . *what?* Every sense in her body was screaming that there was something wrong here.

"Have you read any of my books?"

It was his voice, she decided. There was danger in his tone. Her eyes flicked over his shoulder . . . and froze. In the open drawer behind Walter she saw a transparent plastic bag with a dress inside. It was strange enough to find a man living alone, a bachelor, with a woman's dress in his drawer. Then Ellie saw that it was a red paisley dress. Exactly like the one Kay Connell had been wearing at the party the night of her death.

She moved her eyes nervously from the drawer to Walter Finch. "I . . ."

Crack! She never had the chance to finish her sentence. Walter backhanded her, a violent blow to her chin. Ellie's vision exploded with bright flashes and she fell backward helplessly onto the floor. She knew she needed to resist, but she was dazed and stupid, overwhelmed with pain. Strong hands took hold of her and dragged her across the floor. Awkwardly, he got his arms underneath hers and hauled her up onto a cot. She felt Finch's fingers explore her body obscenely until he found her gun, her Glock 40.

Ellie lay on the cot dizzy with pain, tasting blood in her mouth. Through the mist of disorien-

tation, she was aware that the mystery writer was
enjoying himself. This was a treat for him, what
Walter liked doing best.

Will Dormer drove north along the coast road
to Umkumiut. Black clouds darkened the sky and
the wind was blowing hard, rocking the Cherokee
as it traveled along the road. He felt calm, almost
steady. It was good to have his gold shield back on
his belt. It made him feel like a cop for the first
time in a long while.

He parked in front of Walter's apartment building and made his way inside. He paused in front
of Walter's door, reaching for his .45. With a sharp
inhalation of breath, he raised his foot and kicked
out violently. The door smashed open. Will entered the room in a crouch, pivoting his gun from
side to side. But the windows were closed and the
place was stuffy, empty of life. He moved cautiously from room to room, taking no chances. The
dogs were gone and there was no sign of Finch.

Will holstered his gun and tried to think. The
apartment felt abandoned. The garbage had
been put out, the dog dishes were in the sink,
and the bed had been stripped. Will recalled that
the writer had another house somewhere, on a
lake. He crossed the living room to a bookshelf
and pulled out a copy of one of Walter's books,
the hardcover edition of *Otherwise Engaged*. On
the back flap there was a small reproduction of

the photo of Finch in profile. The caption underneath read, *Walter Finch at his summer house on
Lake Kgun.*

It was impossible to say for certain, but it
would certainly be a smart move for Finch to go to
his summer house for a while, keeping out of
sight and away from Will's wrath, until Will made
it safely back to L.A. Will unfolded his road map
and began searching among all the thousands of
Alaskan lakes for Lake Kgun. He found it first in
the index, then lined up the coordinates until the
name popped in front of his eyes. Lake Kgun
wasn't far from Nightmute, maybe fifty or sixty
miles.

Will was refolding the road map when he noticed a stack of letters on the desk. He flipped
through them and saw they were all addressed to
Walter Finch in a familiar neatly rounded script.
The return address in the upper right-hand corner
was Kay Connell's.

Will was staring at the letters when a vague
anxiety began creeping up his spine. Wasn't Walter supposed to give these letters to Ellie?

Will's mind moved in a logical progression,
from Ellie to Walter, from point A to point C:

A) Walter Finch had a thing about young
   women, seeking adulation and control.
B) Walter Finch also had a thing about cops.

C) Ergo, Walter Finch would find Ellie Burr
   very attractive indeed.

By the time Will Dormer had arrived at point C,
he was already in motion, running from the apartment to the Jeep outside.

TWENTY-EIGHT

Will drove into the mountains, into a mist of drizzle against his windshield. The wipers slashed back and forth, hypnotically, which was not good for a man who had gone six nights without sleep. His eyes burned, itchy with exhaustion. He opened his side window, hoping the air would rouse him.

Up ahead, the road curved like a coiled snake. He was all right, though. He just had to *concentrate* . . . study the road with extra effort . . . keep himself from drifting off. The mountain mist was as thick as sleep. The road blurred and seemed to curve off in two different directions at once. Will blinked furiously, forcing the road back into some semblance of reality.

I'm okay, he told himself. *Been driving my whole*

fucking life! Then suddenly there were headlights coming at him, out of nowhere. Will cranked the wheel hard to the left. His tires screamed. He spun almost lazily, a full 360 degrees. The Cherokee slammed into the guardrail and shuddered to a stop.

At least it woke him up. Will stared through the windshield, his heart thumping crazily, looking for the car that had run him off the road. But there was nothing. No goddamn car, no headlights, only a deserted mountain road! He slammed the Cherokee back into gear and peeled off along the highway, a ferocious grin on his face. It was like the bumper sticker hippies put on their cars in California: I BRAKE FOR HALLUCINATIONS.

He had to do better than this. He worked on keeping his concentration sharp. When he felt he was about to lose it, he stuck his head out of the window into the howling air. He kept going over the pass until the road descended into a kind of natural bowl surrounded by mountains. He could see a lake, and across the lake, there were mountains and a glacier. It was like a photograph from a calendar—it was that scenic. Will kept going. It was a piece of cake now. He stopped at a post office, showed his shield, and received directions to Walter Finch's house.

Will saw Ellie Burr's pickup truck in the dirt turnaround by the house. He parked alongside it and approached the house warily, his .45 in hand, crouching and moving fast. The two dogs, Lucy and Desi, came bounding out from around the corner of the house, but he didn't pay them any mind. The dogs were friendly and only wanted to play. He couldn't say that about their master.

He peered into a downstairs window, but saw no one, only a half-furnished room. He tried the front door and found it was unlocked. He slipped inside and stood very still just inside the door, listening hard. The house was deathly quiet, except for the wind crackling the plastic window covers. Tightening his grip on the .45, he moved from the entryway into a hall that was dark and narrow.

Will was stepping softly down the hall when he heard a voice behind him.

"She *knows*, Will."

He spun around, pointing his gun. It was Finch standing near the end of the hall from where Will had just come. The author looked relaxed, almost as though he were happy to see him.

"Where is she?" Will demanded.

"She knows you killed Hap. If you weren't so fucking strung out you'd have realized yourself. I saw it at the questioning. The way she was watching you—"

"Where is she, Finch?" Will stepped forward and raised his gun.

"Calm down, Will." Walter took a step backward. "I've got it under control."

"She has nothing to do with this!"

"She has *everything* to do with this. What's wrong with you? She tells anyone you're fucked. Everything you've worked for, destroyed—get it?"

Will felt a wave of disorientation, his eyes twitching with exhaustion. "Stay there. *Right* there," he ordered. "I'm searching this fucking place."

"For what?"

"The dress."

"Whose dress?"

"Ellie . . ."

"Ellie? What are you talking about?"

He didn't mean Ellie. *He was losing it.* He tried to think. "Kay's dress. And Ellie's here."

Walter smiled. "Kay, Ellie? You're rambling, Will. Like a madman. Lucky you've got me looking out for us."

"What *us*, Finch?" Will asked dangerously.

Walter eyed the gun and stumbled backward. "Stop acting like a lunatic!"

Before Will could stop him, Finch ducked around the corner. Will lurched after him. He ran into the living room, but the writer had vanished. Will was panting for breath, confused, when he sensed motion just to the left of his vision. Walter had been waiting for him, hidden at the side of the door. Will spun around and tried to raise his gun, but he wasn't fast enough. Walter had a saw in his hand and he was bringing it down hard, slashing into Will's right arm. Will felt a shock of pain as the saw bit into his flesh. He staggered, dropping his .45 onto the floor.

Walter began pummeling Will's head with his fists, hitting him again and again, enraged. Just the way he had killed Kay Connell, Will thought vaguely as he slumped to the floor in a pool of his own blood. Helplessly, he was aware of Finch bringing his foot back. Then . . . *crack!* A shoe kicked him in the ribs.

"You should've left, Will . . ."

Another kick, this time to the kidneys. Will coughed blood, dizzy with pain. He knew his .45 was somewhere on the floor, and it was his last chance. He looked about wildly and spotted it, not far away. He was reaching for the gun, fingers stretching toward the cold metal. But Finch got there first. He kicked it away, sending it skidding across the bare wood floor. Will's last chance gone.

"Should've let me take care of things," he heard the writer say.

Ellie Burr opened her eyes, sick to her stomach. Her chin ached, she hurt all over, and she was bleeding in several places. At first she couldn't remember what had happened to her, a temporary memory loss, her consciousness shutting down. Then it all came back to her. Walter Finch! My God, she had walked right into his trap!

Ellie sat up carefully. She was in the upstairs

room, Finch's office, but everything was woozy. She was tempted to just lie back and sleep, but anger kept her going. Anger at herself for being so stupid, anger at the man who had hurt her, and anger at Will Dormer for not living up to her image of him. She stood up slowly and reached to her holster for her gun . . . but it was gone! She remembered the writer's hands all over her, invasive, taking the Glock. Downstairs she could hear sounds of two people fighting, a thumping of bodies and cries of pain. *Who?* Finch and . . . *Will?*

She reached for the doorknob, but the door was locked. If she was to live, she knew she had to get out of that room. Ellie looked around desperately. The window was her only hope. She ripped back the plastic and climbed out onto a slanting roof, which was slippery from the drizzle. The roof continued for about five feet and came to an abrupt end, overhanging the back porch below. The distance to the ground was ten or eleven feet—it looked even farther, but there was no other option. Ellie dangled her feet over the edge, slid down as far as she could manage, then leaped out toward a small shrub below.

Ooomph! She landed on the hard ground and fell backward onto her ass. The pain of all her earlier injuries screamed in protest, added to the new pain. For a few moments she could only sit there, breathing and wanting to cry. She forced herself to stand. She could hear the struggle going on in the living room. The front door was hanging open. Cautiously, she stepped close to the door and peered inside. Finch was standing over a figure who was prone on the floor, kicking him repeatedly. The man on the floor was Will Dormer, groaning with each new assault. Finch was like a madman, enjoying himself, methodical. But he hadn't seen her yet.

Ellie saw that there was a gun on the floor. It was Dormer's .45 automatic lying near a bureau about a dozen feet from where the men were fighting. Could she get to it before Finch spotted her and got there first. *You bet I can!*

Ellie leaped from the door. She ran two steps, then rolled onto the floor, coming up with the .45 in her hand. Finch was trying to rush her, but he had seen her too late. She fired while still in motion, rolling to her feet. The shot missed, but it convinced Finch to stop his charge and run from the room, disappearing down the hall.

She saw that Dormer was struggling to his feet. He looked terrible. His right arm was slick with blood. But Ellie didn't trust him, not even when he was hurt.

"Don't move!" she ordered, aiming the .45 at his chest. He stared at her with unfocused eyes, confused to find her holding a gun on him. Even now she found him intimidating. But Ellie wasn't backing down.

"You shot Detective Eckhart!" Her voice was bitter with the terrible force of her disillusionment.

Will stood holding his bleeding arm, wobbly with pain. Very slowly, deliberately, he nodded his head. The simple truthfulness of the nod surprised her.

"Did you mean to?" she asked.

Will looked around the room, as though he were searching for an answer. When he spoke, his voice was strangely gentle.

"I don't know anymore. I couldn't see through the fog . . . but when I got to Hap . . . he was *afraid* of me. Maybe somehow I let it happen. Maybe I wanted it . . . but could I have *done* it?"

Will himself didn't seem to know the answer. He looked at her mutely, appealing for help, as though only she could decide this confusing matter.

"He *knew* me," he went on, tortured with doubt. "And he thought I could. . . . I just don't know anymore."

Ellie studied him. There was something utterly honest about Will's uncertainty. He wavered on his feet, reaching out for the wall to steady himself. Her judgment wavered as well. She still didn't know.

Without warning, there came a deafening explosion, a blast from a shotgun. *Boom!* The plastic covering the window ripped inward. Ellie and

Will dove to the floor. She had almost forgotten Walter Finch.

Boom! There was another blast from the shotgun. Finch was somewhere outside the house firing at them. Plaster fell from the ceiling, filling the room with white dust. Ellie shielded her face with her hands. Will was a few feet away, kneeling on the far side of the window, looking at her, still waiting for her judgment.

Ellie slid the .45 over to him, sending it skittering across the floor. At this point, both of them bleeding and hurt, it was hard to say exactly where justice lay. But she knew she needed to trust Will Dormer if either of them was going to get out of this alive.

TWENTY-NINE

Will grabbed hold of the .45 and peered over the windowsill, keeping low. Directly across from them, there was a dilapidated wooden boathouse by the water, a structure that was halfway in ruins about fifty feet from the main house. There was a gaping window in the side of the boathouse that was nearest them, a square opening that had no glass. Will was almost certain that this was where Walter Finch was firing from. The two dogs, Lucy and Desi, were crouched near the boathouse door, staying close to their master.

Will slid back from the window. The movement caused him to wince in pain. Blood was still gushing from his right arm. He crawled along the wall beneath the window to where Ellie was kneeling. Another shotgun blast ripped through the windowframe. Will pushed Ellie's head down. Wood splintered like shrapnel, flying through the air.

"Where's your gun?" he asked, seeing her holster was empty.

"I don't know. He took it."

Will tried to think through the gathering haze of pain, wondering what choices they had. It would have been a big help if he'd brought his 9mm Walther along instead of packing it last night. That backup gun was proving unlucky even now; without it, he and Ellie had only one weapon between them. He checked the magazine in the .45. There were six bullets left, which was not a cause for optimism. Not against someone with a shotgun who might have virtually unlimited ammunition.

He glanced about the living room, hoping to find some way out of their predicament. At the far end of the room, a door opened onto a back porch that appeared to be in even worse shape than the rest of this run-down dump—rotten floorboards where a person would need to step very carefully. Still, the porch couldn't be seen from the boathouse. . . .

Will turned his attention back to Ellie. "Get over to the window," he told her, nodding toward a window in the corner of the living room farthest from the back porch. "Start shooting at the boathouse. Keep your head down. He's going to shoot back." Will handed her the .45.

Ellie swallowed hard and nodded. Will watched as she scurried on her hands and knees to the corner window, crouching next to the sill. She gave him a final look that lingered with many unsaid things. Then she got down to business. She raised her head carefully, pointed the .45 out the window, and fired off a shot. *Bam!*

Will didn't waste time. Keeping close to the floor, he crawled across the living room onto the back porch. The boards there were worse than he had judged, rotten from decades of dampness and nesting insects. He made his way to a jagged hole in the floor and smashed his foot down into the gap, splintering the wood to make the gap large enough for him to fit through. It took only a moment; then he slipped down from the porch into a forest of wooden stilts and bare ground.

Boom! Finch had just fired from the boathouse, the deep bass of his shotgun echoing against the mountains. *Bam!* This was a treble shot, lighter and closer by, obviously Ellie with the .45. Will ignored the gunfire and made his way among the stilts beneath the back porch. The lake was nearby, lapping against the rocky shore, only a few feet beyond where the porch ended. Will crawled past the end of the house and slipped into shallow water, which was bitterly cold, making him catch his breath. It was raining harder, puckering the surface of the lake. Will waded away from the shore and began making his way toward the dilapidated old dock that stuck out from the rear of the boathouse into the water. He pulled himself beneath the dock, moving through the rotten pylons, then swam in a silent breaststroke toward the back of the boathouse, careful to keep his head down.

The lake numbed his pain. The water was like liquid ice, only marginally warmer than the glacier that fed it. Will swam to a narrow walkway at the rear of the boathouse and tried to pull himself up, but the wood was so rotten it fell apart in his hand. He floated down another couple of feet and found a better place where there was a more solid beam to hold him. With a huge effort, he pulled himself up out of the water onto the walkway. The pain in his right arm returned in a rush, leaving him gasping for breath. Will forced himself on. There was a window above him, another empty frame without glass. He reached for the sill and used it to help him get to his feet. Through the opening, he could see Walter Finch standing with his back to him at the far window facing the house. Finch was reloading his shotgun with a box of shells open on a worktable.

Suddenly there was a shot from the main house. *Bam!* A bullet whizzed by him, inches from his left ear—Ellie's bullet, probably one of her last. Will watched as Finch raised the shotgun, aimed out the window, and fired back. *Boom!* The noise of the gunfire was helpful for Will, covering his own sounds as he climbed over the sill. He was lowering himself as quietly as he was able onto the boathouse floor when . . . *damn!* Suddenly Luci and Desi began to howl, barking up a storm. Will had forgotten about the dogs.

Finch whipped around, surprised. Will leaped from the window and charged him before he could bring his shotgun all the way around. He smashed the writer against the wall. The wall behind Finch splintered loudly as it took his weight, nearly breaking through. Will's fury gave him strength. He punched at Walter's head with his right hand, while grabbing at the shotgun with his left, trying to wrench it away. Walter stumbled, but he refused to give up the gun. He had recovered from his surprise and was fighting back, pounding on Will's injured shoulder.

Will twisted his body and kicked out viciously with his left foot. Finch hurtled backward against the worktable. Will threw himself on the other man, refusing to give the writer time to recover. It was a tough fight. They were in close quarters and it was difficult for either of them to land a decisive blow. Finch had his shotgun by the barrel and was trying to use it as a club. Will felt the stock of the shotgun slam against his head. It was a solid hit. Dizzily, he saw the gun was coming at him again. But this time Will managed to get inside the swing and tear the shotgun away with his hand. The gun clattered to the floor. Will was about to launch himself on Finch when he felt the floor give way beneath him. His leg crashed through a rotten board.

He was stuck, helpless.

With calm deliberation, Finch came forward and set to work. The writer hit Will again and again, raining punishing blows down upon him. Will couldn't get free from the rotten floorboard to defend himself. He thought he was finished. With all his remaining strength, he aimed a final blow at Walter's chin . . . *connecting!* Walter reeled backward, crashed against the wall, and slid onto the floor.

Will jerked his leg out from the rotten board and grabbed the shotgun from the floor. Broken and bloody, he limped closer to where Finch was sprawled on the floor. It was over now. Finally over.

But Finch looked up at him and smiled. "You forgot the wild card, Will."

Will's eyes opened wide, understanding. Finch's hand was in his coat pocket. Of course! He had . . . *Ellie's gun!*

Will swung the shotgun around and pulled the trigger. They fired at the same time and the explosions were deafening, the Glock 40 and the shotgun going off in unison. Will felt a huge force lift him backward, ripping into his chest. He fell onto the floor, dreamily. The pain was remote. It was almost as if this were happening to someone else.

Finch was walking toward him now, unhurt, the Glock in his hand to finish Will off. Will's shot had missed! He fought the numbness that was spreading over him and raised the shotgun. *Click!* He pulled the trigger, but there was no explosion, no shot. The gun was empty. Will had no more defenses left. He watched helplessly as the writer staggered closer. There was a stunned expression on Finch's face and he held the Glock loosely in his hand. Something was wrong with him . . . but what?

Will's eyes moved down Finch's body. He saw there was a stain of blood blossoming across the writer's gut. Will's shot hadn't missed after all! Finch himself appeared only just to notice. He looked down at his stomach and touched the blood, fascinated. Then his eyes looked back up to Will and he began to stagger sideways.

To Will, it all seemed to happen in slow motion. There was a crack of splitting wood and the floor opened up. With a cry, Walter Finch fell down through the rotten wood into the icy water below. Will wasn't sure at first where Walter had gone. He dragged himself to the hole and peered down into the dark green water beneath the boathouse.

Finch was staring up at him. Only his head was visible. His eyes seemed to be pleading for mercy, for help, for understanding. . . . Will wasn't really sure which. Then the writer sank into the murky green and disappeared. Will watched until the thin stream of bubbles ceased and he knew for certain that Walter Finch was truly dead.

THIRTY

Will staggered out of the boathouse onto the dock. Rain was pelting down from a steel-gray sky. It felt good. He raised his face to it and let it wash the blood from his skin. He hoped to make his way slowly to the Jeep and get the hell away from there, but that was optimistic. He had simply run out of strength. The gray sky swirled and went dizzy on him. He sank to his knees, dropping the shotgun. With a sigh, he fell backward onto the rain-slick wood.

"Detective Dormer!"

He heard footsteps running his way. It was Ellie Burr. Will squinted up into the rain and made out her face hovering above him. He couldn't believe she was still here. He managed a kind of half smile.

She knelt down next to him, pulling off her vest to cover him.

"I called for backup. . . ." She stopped, midsentence, seeing the amount of blood on his chest, the seriousness of his wound. "They'll be here soon."

Ellie rocked back on her heels, thinking hard, never taking her eyes from his face. After a moment, she pulled the 9mm shell casing from her pocket, took it from the Ziploc bag, and held it close to his face so he could see.

"Nobody needs to know," she told him. "You didn't mean to do it. I know that even if you don't."

With difficulty, Will focused his eyes to see her. He watched as she turned abruptly to face the lake, cranking her arm back to throw the shell away. He grabbed her wrist, stopping her.

"No!"

Ellie was startled by his sudden strength. She turned from the lake to look at him.

"Don't," he said. "Don't lose your way."

Ellie stared into his eyes, then slowly nodded her agreement. It was enough for Will to know that. His grip loosened on her wrist and his arm dropped. He tried to tell her something, but he could only manage a whisper.

"What?" she asked, leaning closer, putting her ear next to his mouth.

"Let me sleep," he whispered.

Will Dormer felt a great peacefulness settling

around him, weighing down his eyelids and limbs. It was as if he were sinking into the softest pillow in the world.

"Just let me sleep. . . ."

Ellie watched Will Dormer's face until all the anguish she had seen in him over the course of the past few days seemed to simply . . . vanish. After some moments, she realized she was alone. Will was dead, free from all pain. She knelt by his side, weeping bitterly. Her fist was balled up with the 9mm shell still inside. She opened her hand and studied the shell strangely, as though it were some foreign object she had never seen before.

A brass bullet casing, spent and empty. A good man who had made a series of small but fatal mistakes. Ellie could still toss the shell into the lake and save the posthumous memory of Will Dormer's official career. But he had told her not to do that, and she respected him far too much to disregard his final wish.

Across the lake, the mountain glacier was silvery in the mist. Ellie slipped the 9mm shell back into the Ziploc evidence bag. At last, she stood from the dock and walked slowly through the rain to her pickup truck to await the noisy onslaught of police vehicles that would soon be there.

● Onyx

Thrilling suspense that has readers on the edge of their seats

PROOF OF LIFE   19552-3
David Robbins, based on the screenplay by Tony Gilroy
When her husband is kidnapped by South American
rebels, there is only one man Alice Bowman can turn to:
hostage negotiator Terry Thorne. Trapped in a deadly
game, Alice puts much more than her husband's life in
Thorne's hands. But Thorne, playing by his own rules,
knows that nothing changes hands when you are waiting
for PROOF OF LIFE.

15 MINUTES   40934-5
*Gary Goldstein, based on the screenplay by
John Herzfeld*
Eddie Fleming, Manhattan's best detective, has built his
his reputation in the tabloids. Jordy Warsaw, an arson
investigator, hates it when showboaters like Eddie try to
"help" him with his job. But a double homicide at a fire
scene forces these two tough cops to work the case together. Now a pair of media savvy psychos, using a stolen
video camera, begin to realize their **15 MINUTES** of fame.

To order call: 1-800-788-6262